WALKING THE DOG
AND OTHER STORIES

by the same author

SECRETS AND OTHER STORIES

LAMB

A TIME TO DANCE AND OTHER STORIES

CAL

THE GREAT PROFUNDO AND OTHER STORIES

WALKING THE DOG

AND OTHER STORIES

Bernard Mac Laverty

JONATHAN CAPE
LONDON

First published 1994

1 3 5 7 9 10 8 6 4 2

© Bernard Mac Laverty 1994

Bernard Mac Laverty has asserted his right
under the Copyright, Designs and Patents Act 1988
to be identified as the author of this work

Walking the Dog was originally published in *Story* magazine, *The Wake House* in
the American edition of *GQ*, and *A Foreign Dignitary* in the *New Statesman*

First published in Great Britain in 1994 by Jonathan Cape
Random House, 20 Vauxhall Bridge Road, London SW1V 2SA

Random House Australia (Pty) Limited
20 Alfred Street, Milsons Point, Sydney,
New South Wales 2061, Australia

Random House New Zealand Limited
18 Poland Road, Glenfield,
Auckland 10, New Zealand

Random House South Africa (Pty) Limited
PO Box 337, Bergvlei, South Africa

Random House UK Limited Reg. No. 954009

A CIP catalogue record for this book
is available from the British Library

ISBN 0–224–03681–5

Typeset by Deltatype Ltd, Ellesmere Port, Cheshire
Printed in Great Britain by
Mackays of Chatham plc, Chatham, Kent

for Claire

CONTENTS

On the Art of the Short Story 1

Walking the Dog 3

The Voyeur 13

The Grandmaster 15

The Fountain-Pen Shop Woman 39

A Silent Retreat 41

Looking out the Window – I 61

At the Beach 63

By Train 109

The Wake House 111

A Visit to Norway 123

In Bed 125

This Fella I Knew 135

A Foreign Dignitary 139

O'Donnell v. Your Man 149

Compensations 151

St Mungo's Mansion 167

Just Visiting 169

Looking out the Window – II 197

ON THE ART OF THE SHORT STORY

'This is a story with a trick beginning.'

Your man put down his pen and considered the possibility that if he left this as the only sentence then his story would also have a trick ending.

WALKING THE DOG

As he left the house he heard the music for the start of the Nine O'Clock news. At the top of the cul-de-sac was a paved path which sloped steeply and could be dangerous in icy weather like this. The snow had melted a little during the day but frozen over again at night. It had done this for several days now – snowing a bit, melting a bit, freezing a bit. The walked-over ice crackled as he put his weight on it and he knew he wouldn't go far. He was exercising the dog – not himself.

The animal's breath was visible on the cold air as it panted up the short slope onto the main road, straining against the leash. The dog stopped and lifted his leg against the cement post.

'Here boy, come on.'

He let him off the leash and wrapped the leather round his hand. The dog galloped away then stopped and turned, not used with the icy surface. He came back wagging his tail, his big paws slithering.

'Daft bugger.'

It was a country road lined by hedges and ditches. Beyond the housing estate were green fields as far as Lisburn. The city had grown out to here within the last couple of years. As yet there was no footpath. Which meant he had to be extra careful in keeping the dog under control. Car headlights bobbed over the hill and approached.

'C'mere!'

He patted his thigh and the dog stood close. Face the oncoming traffic. As the car passed, the undipped headlights turned the dog's eyes swimming-pool green. Dark filled in again between the hedges. The noise of the car took a long time to disappear completely. The dog was now snuffling and sniffing at everything in the undergrowth – being the hunter.

The man's eyes were dazzled as another car came over the hill.

'C'mere you.' The dog came to him and he rumpled and patted the loose folds of skin around its neck. He stepped into the ditch and held the dog close by its collar. This time the car indicated and slowed and stopped just in front of him. The passenger door opened and a man got out and swung the back door wide so that nobody could pass on the inside. One end of a red scarf hung down the guy's chest, the other had been flicked up around his mouth and nose.

'Get in,' the guy said.

'What?'

'Get in the fuckin car.' He was beckoning with one hand and the other was pointing. Not pointing but aiming a gun at him. Was this a joke? Maybe a starting pistol.

'Move or I'll blow your fuckin head off.' The dog saw the open door and leapt up into the back seat of the car. A voice shouted from inside,

'Get that hound outa here.'

'Come on. Get in,' said the guy with the gun. 'Nice and slow or I'll blow your fuckin head off.'

Car headlights were coming from the opposite direction. The driver shouted to hurry up. The guy with the gun grabbed him by the back of the neck and pushed – pushed his head down and shoved him into the car. And he was in the back seat beside his dog with the gunman crowding in beside him.

'Get your head down.' He felt a hand at the back of his neck forcing his head down to his knees. The headlights of the approaching car lit the interior for a moment – enough to see that the upholstery in front of him was blue – then everything went dark as the car passed. He could hear his dog panting. He felt a distinct metal hardness – a point – cold in the nape hair of his neck.

'If you so much as move a muscle I'll kill you. I will,' said the gunman. His voice sounded as if it was shaking with nerves. 'Right-oh driver.'

'What about the dog?' said the driver.

'What about it? It'd run home. Start yapping, maybe. People'd start looking.'

'Aye, mebby.'

'On you go.'

'There's something not right about it. Bringing a dog.'

'On you fuckin go.'

The car took off, changed gear and cruised – there seemed to be no hurry about it.

'We're from the IRA,' said the gunman. 'Who are you?'

There was a silence. He was incapable of answering.

'What's your name?'

He cleared his throat and made a noise. Then said, 'John.'

'John who?'

'John Shields.'

'What sort of a name is that?'

It was hard to shrug in the position he was in. He had one foot on either side of the ridge covering the main drive shaft. They were now in an area of street lighting and he saw a Juicy Fruit chewing-gum paper under the driver's seat. What was he playing the detective for? The car would be stolen anyway. His hands could touch the floor but were around his knees. He still had the dog's lead wrapped round his fist.

'Any other names?'

'What like?'

'A middle name.'

The dog had settled and curled up on the seat beside him. There was an occasional bumping sound as his tail wagged. The gunman wore Doc Martens and stone-washed denims.

'I said, any other names?'

'No.'

'You're lying in your teeth. Not even a Confirmation name?'

'No.'

'What school did you go to?'

There was a long pause.

'It's none of your business.' There was a sudden staggering pain in the back of his head and he thought he'd been shot. 'Aww – for fuck's sake.' The words had come from him so he couldn't be dead. The bastard must have hit him with the butt of the gun.

'No cheek,' said the gunman. 'This is serious.'

'For fuck's sake, mate – take it easy.' He was shouting and groaning and rubbing the back of his head. The anger in his voice raised the dog and it began to growl. His fingers were slippery. The blow must have broken the skin.

'Let me make myself clear,' said the gunman. 'I'll come to it in one. Are you a Protestant or a Roman Catholic?'

There was a long pause. John pretended to concentrate on the back of his neck.

'That really fuckin hurt,' he said.

'I'll ask you again. Are you a Protestant or a Roman Catholic?'

'I'm . . . I don't believe in any of that crap. I suppose I'm nothing.'

'You're a fuckin wanker – if you ask me.'

John protected his neck with his hands thinking he was going to be hit again. But nothing happened.

'What was your parents?'

'The same. In our house nobody believed in anything.'

The car slowed and went down the gears. The driver indicated and John heard the rhythmic clinking as it flashed. This must be the Lisburn Road. A main road. This was happening on a main road in Belfast. They'd be heading for the Falls. Some Republican safe house. The driver spoke over his shoulder.

'Let's hear you saying the alphabet.'

'Are you serious?'

'Yeah – say your abc's for us,' said the gunman.

'This is so fuckin ridiculous,' said John. He steeled himself for another blow.

'Say it – or I'll kill you.' The gunman's voice was very matter-of-fact now. John knew the myth that Protestants and Roman Catholics, because of separate schooling, pronounced the eighth letter of the alphabet differently. But he couldn't remember who said which.

'Eh . . . bee . . . cee, dee, ee . . . eff.' He said it very slowly, hoping the right pronunciation would come to him. He stopped.

'Keep going.'

'Gee . . .' John dropped his voice, '. . . aitch, haitch . . . aye jay kay.'

'We have a real smart Alec here,' said the gunman. The driver spoke again.

'Stop fuckin about and ask him if he knows anybody in the IRA who can vouch for him.'

'Well?' said the gunman. 'Do you?'

There was another long pause. The muzzle of the gun touched his neck. Pressure was applied to the top bone of his vertebrae.

'Do you?'

'I'm thinking.'

'It's not fuckin Mastermind. Do you know anybody in the Provos? Answer me now or I'll blow the fuckin head off you.'

'No,' John shouted. 'There's a couple of guys in work who are Roman Catholics – but there's no way they're Provos.'

'Where do you work?'

'The Gas Board.'

'A meter man?'

'No. I'm an E.O.'

'Did you hear that?' said the gunman to the driver.

'Aye.'

'There's not too many Fenians in the Gas Board.'

'Naw,' said the driver. 'If there are any they're not E.O. class.
I think this is a dud.'

'John Shields,' said the gunman. 'Tell us this. What do you
think of us?'

'What do you mean?'

'What do you think of the IRA? The Provos?'

'Catch yourselves on. You have a gun stuck in my neck and
you want me to . . .'

'Naw – it'd be interesting. Nothing'll happen – no matter
what you say. Tell us what you think.'

There was silence as the car slowed down and came to a
stop. The reflections from the chrome inside the car became
red. Traffic lights. John heard the beeping of a 'cross now'
signal. For the benefit of the blind. Like the pimples on the
pavement. To let them know where they were.

'Can you say the Hail Mary? To save your bacon?'

'No – I told you I'm not interested in that kind of thing.'

The driver said,

'I think he's okay.'

'Sure,' said the gunman. 'But he still hasn't told us what he
thinks of us.'

John cleared his throat – his voice was trembling.

'I hate the Provos. I hate everything you stand for.' There was a pause. 'And I hate you for doing this to me.'

'Spoken like a man.'

The driver said,

'He's no more a Fenian than I am.'

'Another one of our persuasion.' The gunman sighed with a kind of irritation. The lights changed from orange to green. The car began to move. John heard the indicator clinking again and the driver turned off the main road into darkness. The car stopped and the hand brake was racked on. The gunman said,

'Listen to me. Careful. It's like in the fairy tale. If you look at us you're dead.'

'You never met us,' said the driver.

'And if you look at the car we'll come back and kill you – no matter what side you're from. Is that clear? Get out.'

John heard the door opening at the gunman's side. The gunman's legs disappeared.

'Come on. Keep the head down.' John looked at his feet and edged his way across the back seat. He bent his head to get out and kept it at that angle. The gunman put his hands on John's shoulders and turned him away from the car. There was a tree in front of him.

'Assume the position,' said the gunman. John placed his hands on the tree and spread his feet. His knees were shaking so much now that he was afraid of collapsing. 'And keep your head down.' The tarmac pavement was uneven where it had been ruptured by the tree's roots. John found a place for his feet.

The dog's claws scrabbled on the metal sill of the car as it followed him out. It nudged against his leg and he saw the big eyes looking up at him. The gunman said,

'Sorry about this, mate.' John saw the gunman's hand reach down and scratch the dog's head. 'Sorry about the thump. But we're not playing games. She's a nice dog.'

'It's not a she.'

'Okay, okay. Whatever you say.'

The car door closed and the car began reversing – crackling away over the refrozen slush. In the headlights his shadow was very black and sharp against the tree. There was a double shadow, one from each headlight. From the high-pitched whine of its engine he knew the car was still reversing. It occurred to him that they would not shoot him from that distance. For what seemed a long time he watched his shadow moving on the tree even though he kept as still as possible. It was a game he'd played as a child, hiding his eyes and counting to a hundred. Here I come, away or not. The headlights swung to the trees lining the other side of the road. His dog was whimpering a bit, wanting to get on. John risked a glance – moving just his eyes – and saw the red glow of the car's tail lights disappearing onto the main road. He recognised where he was. It was the Malone Road. He leaned his head against the back of his hands. Even his arms were trembling now. He took deep breaths and put his head back to look up into the branches of the tree.

'Fuck me,' he said out loud. The sleeve of his anorak had slipped to reveal his watch. It was ten past nine. He began to unwind the leash from his hand. It left white scars where it had bitten into his skin. He put his hand to the back of his head. His hair was sticky with drying blood.

'Come on boy.' He began to walk towards the lights of the main road where he knew there was a phone box. But what was the point? He wouldn't even have been missed yet.

The street was so quiet he could hear the clinking of the dog's identity disk as it padded along beside him.

THE VOYEUR

At night your man dresses for exercise. A navy track suit, thick-soled trainers to give bounce to his step. In the winter he wears woollen gloves. In summer he discards the track suit top for a vest. Your man runs, knowing all the time it's not his body which is the cause for concern.

In the darkness as he pants along city streets he looks for lit windows. In a street he knows of old he stops and stares into basements. He sees men, sometimes women, sitting at desks in a pool of light from an anglepoise, writing – sometimes reading. He stands, his breath returning slowly to normal, and, with wide eyes, watches the scene.

Sometimes little dramas are enacted in front of him and his breathing almost disappears. To see the reader or the writer interrupted – for the man or woman to be absorbed in what they're doing and be disturbed by their partner or spouse or friend – that, for him, is something special. They may have poor eyesight and have to put their glasses to one side to regard the interrupter – either by tilting them to the top of the head or dropping them to the middle of the chest to hang on a chain. The person who has been disturbed sighs with irritation at the loved one. Must you interrupt me, they seem to say. With *finger and thumb they may massage the bridge of the nose, skin irritated by long contact with the spectacles. Or they stretch and yawn and engage in double-handed head scratching. They know they should stop – they have overdone it for one day. Too much bloody work, they seem to say.*

THE GRANDMASTER

The lights beside the hotel swimming-pool were turned out at midnight. One moment Isobel was staring down from the ninth floor and the next there was nothing but darkness and the sound of crickets. She pulled the curtains and undressed for bed.

The knickers she was wearing were smaller than her bikini bottoms so she could see in the full-length mirror a margin of Scottish pale around her waist and groin. Everything else was red. Including her breasts.

'Jesus – how utterly . . .'

Her blood throbbed. She slipped a cotton nightdress over her head and gently lowered herself onto the bed nearest the window. For a while she attempted to read but could not concentrate. Then she switched out the light and tried to sleep. In the dark she felt she could take her pulse on any part of her exposed skin. The hotel radio had a digital clock which now showed one sixteen and still there was no sign of her daughter. She blew on her arms and it soothed them momentarily.

She began to shiver. It came in waves. When she tensed it was difficult to control. If she relaxed the teeth-chattering stopped briefly. She switched on the light, got up and found a strip of paracetamol in her wash-bag and punched out two from the foil, swallowing them with a swig of bottled water.

Within a few moments she was too hot again. She soaked a towel and took it to bed with her. She dabbed her face and shoulders and down the front of her nightdress between her breasts. Her watch on the bedside table agreed with the radio clock.

'Damn and blast her.'

Isobel was lying on her bed, trying not to make contact with any of it, when Gillian came in. The girl didn't even look at her.

'Where on earth have you been?'

'The disco.'

'Oh – I'm glad you were somewhere safe. An English lager lout or two . . . Do you know what time it is?'

The girl shook her head, went into the bathroom and closed the door. Isobel heard the taps running and the flushing and the teeth-brushing. When Gillian came out she was in her pyjamas with her hair in a pony-tail.

'For your information it's two o'clock, girl.'

Gillian looked over at the digital clock.

'It's one fifty-two,' she said and got into her bed. She pulled the sheet up over her shoulder and turned her face to the wall.

'Who with?'

'Who with what?'

'Captain Plum . . . in the Library . . . with a bloody spanner. I mean who did you go to the disco with?'

'Everybody.'

'Oh I'm glad everybody was there – everybody who?'

'Everybody from here. Give over, Mum. We're on our holidays.'

'Don't you talk to me like that, Gillian. There's not too many thirteen-year-olds who'd be allowed out to this time of the morning.'

'I came home *early*, for God's sake. Everybody's away on somewhere else. I feel such a baby.' Gillian put on a childish voice. ' "I have to go home. My mammy says." '

Isobel gave a sigh and said,

'You were okay the day you were born but it's been downhill ever since.' Gillian pulled the sheet up over her head. 'I'll come with you next night.'

'No way.'

'D'you think I'd cramp your style?' The girl didn't answer. 'Did it ever occur to you that *you* might be cramping *my* style?'

Gillian shrugged beneath her sheet. 'What are you on about?'

'Gillian – just promise me one thing – never marry a physics teacher.' Isobel began to make small sniffing noises. Her daughter hesitated, wondering if this was tears. Isobel said,

'You've been smoking again.'

'Honest no.'

'I can smell it, Gillian.'

'Piss off, Mum.'

'That kind of language may make your father laugh – but not me.'

'Everybody else smokes. It just gets in your clothes from the bar.'

'Gillian?'

'What?'

'Look at me and tell me you haven't been smoking.'

With a sigh of irritation the girl turned in her bed to face the room. 'Jesus – Mum.' Gillian was aghast, laughing. She sat up, her elbow on her pillow. 'What a face! You're puce – positively puce.'

'That is not the issue at the moment. We're talking death by smoking – not skin cancer.' Isobel's voice had dropped, her daughter's rose with incredulity.

'Everyday this week you've been moaning on and on and on at *me* not to get too much sun . . .'

'One time I got really badly burnt . . .'

'But you've been wearing factor a zillion.'

'Not today I wasn't. I want a tan too.'

'You've really overdone it.'

'Just a tad, dear. Just a tad.'

'Is it sore?'

'Hot.' Her chin began to shiver.

'Are you all right?'

'Yeah,' said Isobel. She slid down in the bed and pulled the sheet up to her neck. 'A bit feverish. But I'll be okay in the morning.'

'Turn out the light?'

'Yeah – I'll look better that way.'

It had been five years since Isobel had shared a bedroom and now, even after a week, she was not used to it – sounds of breathing, of springs twanging at each turn, the slither of sheets being pulled up or kicked away. Later her daughter's heavy breathing or snoring would keep her awake. All she could do then was lie and stare at the bedroom wall in the light from the digital clock. At home she could have gone down and made hot milk or something. When neither of them could sleep, both were aware of it. The sound of steady breathing was absent, twisting and turning became more frequent the longer they did not sleep, there was a sound of yawning.

'Mum?'

'What?'

'Are you asleep?'

'Yes – I'm absolutely sound.'

'You know that hotel at the far end of the beach?'

'The maroon one?'

'Naw – next to it – The Corvo or something.'

'Mm-mm.'

'They have chess in there.'

'I suppose it makes a change from playing pool.'

'There's a guy plays twelve people at once. He's great.'

'How many hands has he got?'

'I was going really well too. Until he took one of my rooks. I was just so *stupid* not to see it coming.'

'I didn't know you could play.'

'I can't wait to get back at him. He just shrugged and took the rook. I couldn't *believe* I'd made a move like that.'

'I presume this was before the disco.'

'Thursday night – I'm going back. It'll be my last chance before we go home.'

Isobel eased herself off the bed and went to the bathroom to cool her face again. A square of light fell on the wall opposite the bathroom. 'I can't go to the beach tomorrow – looking like this.' Isobel turned out the light and groped her way to her bed. She lay down and started blowing on her skin.

'I wish I'd some calamine.'

'I've got some.'

'I don't believe it. You angel.' Gillian got out of bed and went to the bathroom. 'Why didn't you bloody tell me sooner?' Isobel switched on the bedside light. Her daughter came from the bathroom with cotton wool and a bottle of pink calamine lotion.

'Thanks,' said Isobel, holding out her hands.

'It's okay. I'll do it for you. Close your eyes.' Isobel lay back on the pillow and heard the thick liquid glug as Gillian upended the bottle onto the cotton wool pad.

'This is not like you, Gillian – to have foresight.' She felt the coolness on her forehead and her eyelids and her cheeks. 'Oh that's lovely.'

'Dad bought it for me last year in Majorca. I just never took it out of my wash-bag.'

'Oh – well despite that – it's working. It's so soothing.'

Gillian changed the cotton wool pad for a fresh one and began again.

'I'd like to work in a beauty parlour or somewhere.'

'I don't think you have the intellectual mettle for it.'

'It's so relaxing.'

'It's me that's supposed to relax – not the therapist.' But Isobel ummed and sighed as the treatment continued.

'What did *you* do tonight?' asked her daughter.

'I hung out with some people in the bar. We chilled out together.'

Gillian snorted and did her mother's arms and the scarlet tip of each shoulder. Isobel started to laugh silently.

'What? Mum, what is it?'

'A terrible rhyme. A little pal o' mine soothed me with calamine.'

'That's the pits. It's awful.'

Isobel felt the bottle being pushed into her hands.

'You can do your boobies yourself,' said Gillian.

Isobel and her daughter sat on the patio of the Hotel Condor, waiting. In the flashing darkness there was a disco on for the very young ones.

'You look a mess.' Isobel had to shout above the noise. 'It's no wonder people think you're a boy.' The girl's hair was cut short and she wore a white T-shirt hanging out over her khaki shorts. Her chest was still very flat. Between records the sound of crickets was incessant.

'And stop that with your nails.' Gillian was gnawing, not her nails, but the skin around her nails. 'Gill – i – an.' The girl took her hand away from her mouth and said,

'What does a cricket look like?'

'It's a beetle kind of thing. I've never seen one.'

'They sound like a herd of telephones.' Gillian stood and went towards the nearest one. Immediately she approached the source of the sound, it stopped.

'They hear you coming.' She went towards another one in a flower-bed at the top of the steps and the same thing happened. The first one started up again. Gillian whirled round.

'Sneak – ee. Show yourself.' She gave up and came down the steps. 'He's late. It said ten o'clock.'

'Are you sure it's the right night?'

'Och Mum – '

'Check the notice.'

'The place is set up.'

Inside in the lounge a group of card tables covered with green baize had been formed into a square in the centre of the room. Other families sat about, drinking or playing cards, their children running in and out to the flashing coloured lights and music of the patio. They all seemed to be Spanish or French – not British, not English-speaking. Isobel stood up and walked into the hotel lobby where the notice board was.

Her daughter followed her. There was a photograph of the chess player beside printed information about him in three languages.

'He looks like a bit of all right.'

'Mum.'

'He's very intense.'

'He's very late,' said Gillian. The information said he was a Grandmaster and the Catalan champion. He would challenge twelve opponents simultaneously two evenings a week. Tuesdays and Thursdays.

They made their way into the lounge where the tables were set up. Gillian pulled a face and sat down in the deep leather armchair, folding her legs up beneath her.

'All the grace of an ironing board,' said Isobel.

The music they were playing at the disco was old-fashioned stuff – the Beatles, Nina Simone – 'My Baby Just Cares for Me', Glen Miller's version of 'Begin the Beguine'. It became louder each time one of the children ran out through the patio doors. When the automatic doors slid shut, it became distant again.

'Where did you learn to play chess?'

'Dad.'

'Oh – I thought maybe they'd taught it in school.' A waiter passed and she ordered a glass of white wine and a Coke for Gillian. 'When, might I ask?'

'I dunno. Over in his place. Days when there was nothing to do. Days when it was raining.'

'I'm surprised he was sober enough . . .'

'Don't say that.'

'It's true but.'

'He's better – a lot better.'

'No matter how hard he tried he could never teach me. I know the moves all right but the overall thing . . . It's the horse that does the L-shape . . .'

'The knight, Mum.'

'I hadn't the patience for it. We had rows, even about that.'

'When you talk about Dad why d'you always use a voice like that?'

'Like what?'

'You know – "We had rows, even about that." '

'I suppose it's a defence mechanism. When you're left like me, defence is the only method of attack.'

Gillian swung her feet onto the marble floor and stood up.

'Where is he?' She went over to the doorway and looked into the lobby. The waiter arrived and set the drinks on the low table. Isobel called her daughter. When Gillian came back she sipped her Coke standing.

'Your sunburn has cooled down a bit,' she said.

'So it should – after forty-eight hours.'

'It'll peel – when we get back home.'

Isobel crossed her legs and her sandal hung from her foot.

'Mum – for God's sake.'

'What have I done now?' Her daughter nodded to the sandalled foot moving in time to the disco music.

'Only old people do that.'

There was a flurry in the hallway and some boys came running with small wooden boxes. They ran up to the square of card tables and set them on the baize. One of the boys had a roll of plastic green-and-white chequered boards which he laid out like place mats, one beside each box. People's heads turned, waiting for the Grandmaster. He came, talking and gesticulating, in the midst of a crowd.

'About bloody time,' said Gillian. She got up and walked to the tables. The lid of each box had a small gouge shaped like a fingernail to help slide it open. Gillian struggled with hers and when it eventually came the plastic chess pieces spilled out all over the table. Isobel pretended to raise her eyebrows and Gillian blushed.

A member of the hotel staff moved one card table aside so that the Grandmaster could get into the middle. The challengers took their seats and began setting up the boards with the white pieces to the inside. The Grandmaster stood in the middle, his hands loosely clasped behind his back. He recognised some of the players from previous nights and smiled at them. His opponents varied greatly in age. One man, smoking a Gauloise, looked like he was in his eighties. Younger family-men joked over their shoulders to their wives and children, their Spanish voices louder than usual with pre-match nerves. Two boys, about ten years of age, had agreed to play as one.

Isobel came to the tables and stood behind her daughter as she set up the pieces.

'He has nice eyes,' she said. 'His eyes make you like him immediately.'

'Mum, don't loom. Sit down somewhere.' Gillian elbowed her haunch but her mother paid no attention – she was staring at the Grandmaster.

He was in his late forties but boyish-looking and very thin. His beard was beginning to grey. He wore a shirt with a Mondrian-like pattern and Levi's held up by a belt with a slightly too ornate buckle. A showman of sorts, an artist, thought Isobel as she smiled and caught his eye.

'This is my daughter in whom I am well pleased.'

'Oh Mum please – please don't,' said Gillian.

But although he didn't understand, the Grandmaster returned Isobel's smile and inclined his head in a kind of salute to Gillian. He checked around to see that all the boards were set up and then went to the first challenger and shook hands. He gave a little smile then made his first move. He did this with all twelve challengers.

Isobel sat down at a little distance to watch. Gillian waited until the Grandmaster came around again to reply with her move. Isobel could not take her eyes off him. His concentration was immense. It would have taken an earthquake to make him look up. When he moved one of his pieces there was an uncertain hovering of his fingers over the pawn or the queen or whatever, a hesitation – then a definite snatching movement, as if to say – how could I have hesitated for so long? There cannot be any other move.

He wore an expensive watch and two gold rings on the same finger – a thin one and a fat one. Sometimes when his hands rested on the table his shoulders were high, almost above his head, his face staring down in concentration at the board. When he captured a man there was a plastic 'tink' as his piece dislodged the one it was taking. Almost a violence – a return to what the game represented – a formalised battle. This happened especially when it came to an exchange with the old man who smoked the Gauloises.

Any time he made a move to put his opponent in check he did not say the word *check* but tapped the black king with a quick movement.

Isobel got herself a glass of white wine. She was getting bored with the chess with its absence of words. The only thing of interest was the Grandmaster.

It amazed her that it was all inside his head, the drama. There was nothing to see. Little or no outward sign. Sometimes his head moved almost imperceptibly, miming the course of an exchange. 'I take you, you take me back.' He was like an anchorite, a holy man. She felt that if he wanted to he could lower his heart-beat despite the noise of the disco, the bustle of the hotel. She drained her wine glass and ordered another.

There was a ripple of applause as the two boys playing as one were checkmated. They knocked down their king and giggled. The Grandmaster smiled and ruffled their heads. They came running to their parents who made much of them. Isobel smiled and made a gesture of silent applause, indicating the boys. The mother leaned forward and said something in Spanish. Isobel shook her head.

'English,' she said. 'I mean Scottish – I just speak English.'

'My English not good,' said the woman. 'A little.' Having said this both women sat forward in their chairs. Then gradually, having nothing more to say, they leaned back and turned again to watch the game. The next time Isobel caught her eye the Spanish woman pointed towards the square of tables.

'¿Your child?'

'Yes.' Isobel nodded vigorously. Gillian had blinkered herself by pressing both hands to the sides of her head and was staring down at the board between her elbows.

'That is my daughter.' As she said it she blushed and smiled.

'¿Daughter?' They seemed surprised. '¿Did you teach her?' The Spanish woman mimed the moving of chessmen.

'No – in school. She learned in school.' Again they remained poised on the edge of their seats but the communication seemed too difficult and gradually they both sagged back to their original positions.

Over the next hour or so several more opponents resigned or were checkmated and the Grandmaster stopped to explain where they had gone wrong or how he had outmanoeuvred them. After the remorselessness of his play he became a teacher – leaning down confidentially, pointing out the sins, advising for the future.

Isobel got up to stretch her legs and walked out onto the patio. It was still warm. There were only about half a dozen children left at the disco, chasing one another rather than dancing. Their parents sat drinking with their backs to the pool, keeping an eye. This crowd was English – words she recognised floated towards her when the music stopped. She gave them a wide berth, walking round the paths on the terracing. The DJ must have run out of records because he began to play the same ones again. The Nina Simone, the Glen Miller.

By the time she went back into the lounge there were only two challengers left. Her daughter and the old man who smoked the Gauloises. The defeated players and their families were gathered round to watch the final stages. The crowd had swelled to fifty or sixty with guests coming back into the hotel at bedtime. Isobel edged her way to a position where she could see her daughter's face.

The Grandmaster made his move against the old man, whose response was to pull another cigarette from the packet lying by his hand on the table. He could see what was unfolding. He tugged a match free from the booklet and lit up. He coughed and his face went bright red. He was shaking his head in disbelief that he should have walked into such a trap. He cursed and surrendered by turning over his king.

Gillian waited for the Grandmaster to turn and face her before making her move. She looked up at him defiantly. He registered no surprise but took a long time before he made his reply. As far as Isobel could see they had equal numbers of pieces left but she could not tell who had the advantage. She watched the spectators' faces, trying to gauge who was winning and, more importantly, when the game would be over. She yawned and looked at her watch.

The disco music stopped and Isobel became aware of smaller sounds – distant coughing, glasses clinking behind the bar, the sneeze as the automatic doors opened and closed. It was now after midnight. The DJ wheeled a trolley containing his turntables and speakers into the lounge to store them for the night. One of the wheels needed oil. It screeched every time it turned.

'Por favor . . . por favor,' whispered the disc jockey. People in the crowd stepped aside to let him through. But neither Gillian nor the Grandmaster looked up from the board.

Some people in the crowd – certainly the parents of the two youngest boys and others they had told – realised that Isobel was the mother of the child player. She yawned again but this time tried not to open her mouth. Gillian made a move. The Grandmaster's fingers went up to his beard as he considered. Isobel felt another yawn rising and proceeded to yawn with her teeth clenched.

After what seemed an endless pause the Grandmaster moved a pawn. Gillian was now taking almost as long to reply. At half past twelve the Grandmaster smiled and raised his eyebrows at Gillian. He said something in Spanish. Gillian looked blankly at him. The Grandmaster turned and looked around the crowd. He called a girl – Spanish-looking, about twenty years of age, and they spoke in Spanish. The girl turned to Gillian.

'This is my father.' She put her hand out to indicate the Grandmaster. 'And I translate for him. My father would like to offer you a draw.'

Gillian was unsure.

'¡Tablas!' said the Grandmaster to the crowd. They burst into applause. They smiled and the clapping went on and on. Isobel joined in. Gillian began to blush – it was as if she had only realised now that people had been watching. The Grandmaster offered his hand and Gillian, still not sure, shook it. The old man who smoked the Gauloises struggled forward and slapped her on the back. He said something in Spanish to

30

the Grandmaster who laughed. Gillian got to her feet. Isobel edged forward and said,

'I suppose congratulations are in order?'

Gillian's face was sullen – she always hated being the centre of attention. The Grandmaster put his arm around his daughter's shoulder. His eyes met Isobel's and he leaned forward to speak. His daughter translated.

'My father says he is very good.'

'Who?'

'Your son. He is very good.'

'It's my daughter.' The Spanish girl turned to her father and explained. He seemed embarrassed and apologetic.

'He says he is very sorry – *she* is very good. Your daughter is very good.'

'Oh, thank you.' Isobel turned to Gillian who was tugging at her elbow.

'Come on, Mum.'

'How good is that?' His daughter, her hand resting on her father's, relayed the question. The Grandmaster shrugged and pushed out his lip.

'Excellent,' he said in English. His daughter listened to what he had to say then translated,

'He means she is *very, very* good. In the world. By any standard.'

'Her father was very good at it. He taught her.' Both the Grandmaster and his daughter looked around, possibly expecting to see the person in question but there was only the eighty-year-old man fussing around the tables.

'But he's not with us here. Fortunately.' Isobel smiled. 'Where can a game like this lead?' He listened to the question and smiled.

'Nowhere,' translated his daughter, 'but she may enjoy it.'

The crowd had now completely dispersed.

On the way back to their own hotel Isobel sensed her daughter's anger. They walked, as always, a little apart – as if they were not with each other. There was something about the way her sandals were slapping the ground.

'And what's wrong with you?'

'I could've won. He's a cheat.'

'What do you mean?'

'He was cheating. I was going to win. I could see a way to win. And I think he saw it too – that's when he offered me a draw.' Gillian was close to tears. 'And that was my last chance. Men cheat. Everybody cheats.'

'I doubt very much if that's true. Besides it's no big deal.'

'It's no big deal? It's no big deal. I'm . . . I . . . oh fucking hell . . .'

'Forgive me not getting worked up about something your father is entirely responsible for.'

'I might have known that was at the back of it.'

'Gillian, he's a Grandmaster. He could see better than *you* that it was going to be a draw.'

'Don't *say* that – I *hate* when you do that. As if I knew nothing. As if I was too young to know *anything*. You don't even know the fucking moves and you're siding with him.'

'Gillian – please. Your language is deteriorating.'

'You do it with everything – teacher knows best – the doctor knows best – Mum knows best.'

'Not another street scene, please.'

'I *hate* people talking down to me.'

'And how many degrees have you got? Maybe you could remove my appendix later on tonight?'

'According to you even Dad knows nothing.'

'Brain cells aren't destroyed overnight, you know. But he's certainly working hard at it.'

'Oh you – you fucking cow. Why'd you . . .'

'How dare you – how dare you call me that.' Isobel swung her open hand at the girl's face. There was the crack of skin to skin. Gillian screamed and ran off into the dark, her sandals slapping the metalled surface of the road.

'Gillian!' Isobel watched her run from the light of one street lamp through shadow to the next. She followed the white T-shirt and saw her daughter turn down the steps to the beach.

'Bloody bloody bloody bloody hell.'

The beach café was closed and the beach was in darkness. There was sufficient moonlight to outline the boats and pedalos and stacked sunbeds. Isobel threaded her way through them to the water's edge. She could see no sign of Gillian. She knew not to shout her name. To the left-hand side of the beach was a jumble of rocks and boulders. She was not sure but she thought she saw a pale patch which could be her daughter. She walked towards the rocks. A cigarette – small as a pinhead from this distance – glowed and went out again. The nearer she got the surer she was it was Gillian. She was squatting on a rock at the height of her mother's head. She inhaled her cigarette and her cupped hand glowed in the dark. The sea slapped in, in small Mediterranean waves.

'I'm sorry.'

'Fuck away off.'

'I lost my temper. I shouldn't have hit you. You are old enough and ugly enough not to be hit.' Isobel turned her back to the rock and leaned her head against it. 'That was my own mother's doing. I swore it would never happen again. I don't know which was worse – being hit or – having to listen. My mother had the most sarcastic tongue I ever heard. I swore it would never happen to me. But being a teacher doesn't help.' She looked up at her daughter. The cigarette glowed again, then came sailing down past her head to hiss out in the sea at her feet.

'Sometimes I say things. Things I don't mean. Things I'm sorry for afterwards. And I don't have the courage to take them back. That's the times I'm most like her. Dearest mother. And I hate myself.' The cigarette butt was white bobbing against the dark water. 'If there is somewhere still open why don't we go and have a drink – talk about this?'

'I said fuck away off.'

'You're becoming a tad repetitive.'

'You just want to suck in with me.'

'Gillian, please. Do me a favour.' Her mother gave a sigh

and said, 'You were okay the day you were born but it's been downhill ever since.'

At the square a small bar was open. Several tables were still out on the pavement and there was a light on inside. Isobel went in and ordered a glass of wine and an orange juice. An old man with spectacles stood at the counter eating *tapas*. He stared at her, his jaws revolving. The boy who served her was good-looking but young. A son more than a lover. Outside she set the drinks on the table and sat down. In the light from the open doorway she could see that Gillian had been crying for a long time – her face looked puffy and sullen. The girl put her feet on a chair, and turned her body away. Isobel offered her a sip of wine but she refused.

'Each generation tries to make a change for the better – however small. To put one particular piece of debris in the bin.'

'Huh – what was yours?'

'My mother and I never talked. Like now.'

'Great. This is just great. What I really wanted. All my dreams fulfilled. Talking to my mother.'

'Believe me, it's better than taking the huff. We were a family of huffers – for days, weeks on end.'

'I would prefer that.'

'Gillian – I know – I think I know your pain – about how difficult things have been.'

'Like fuck, you do.' Isobel put her hand out to touch the girl's arm but Gillian pulled away and began to search in the pocket of her shorts. She took out a packet of Gauloises and a book of Hotel Condor matches. She tapped a cigarette on the table and lit up.

'That's another thing we should talk about.'

'What?'

'Smoking.'

'Why?'

'Because it kills people.'

'Good.' She inhaled deeply and blew two streams of smoke down her nose. 'That's what it's for.'

'Remember the sticker on the front door – My Mum's a smoker buster. It was the hardest thing I ever did – giving it up. To please you.'

'Gee – thanks.'

'We can get around to talking about stealing from old men some other time.'

'I didn't steal them. He just left them on the table.'

The man who'd been eating the *tapas* came out of the doorway and wandered up the cobbled street a little unsteadily. There was a cricket nearby ringing at great volume.

'That's your story.'

'Shut the fuck up,' Gillian yelled. Then she started laughing. 'I mean the insect – not you, Mum.' Her mother smiled.

'My own mother used to say that it gave her great pleasure to say to people "This is my daughter". Well tonight I understood that. I think I even blushed at one point.'

'Are you taking the piss? Is that sarcastic?'

'No. I felt proud of you. Maybe for the first time.'

'But it was Dad taught me. Nothing to do with you.'

'I felt proud of you despite the fact that the chess was *his* doing. The Glasgow grandmaster. I suppose you can't wait to tell him.'

'What?'

'About the draw.'

'It's none of your business.'

'Gillian – help me to like you.'

'But I don't *want* you to like me. I hate myself – how can anybody else like me.' Her chin began to flex and the girl cried again. 'The whole thing is so fucking stupid. Five years of fucking stupidness.'

Isobel put her arm around her shoulder expecting her to flinch away but she did not. She felt the shakes of her crying and patted her shoulder.

'Where's the calamine?' she said and smiled. They both sat for a long time not saying anything – the night filled with the sound of crickets.

THE FOUNTAIN-PEN SHOP WOMAN

Your man sent his fountain-pen away to be repaired. The fountain-pen shop woman said it would take ten days. The flange and the barrel had somehow become detached and the whole ensemble was liable to flood the breast pocket of his summer linen jacket at any minute. He felt relieved that the responsibility of serious writing was removed from him for the best part of a fortnight. Of course he could work in pencil or biro but it was not the same thing as the oul fountain-pen.

How and ever, when the ten days was up didn't he return to the fountain-pen shop only to find that there was a charge for the repair of the instrument which, the leaflet had said, was guaranteed for life. The fountain-pen shop woman said,

'How can anything to do with writing be guaranteed for life?'

A SILENT RETREAT

The game was almost over. A boy coming in from the wing chipped the ball over the goalkeeper's head and it bounced between the posts.

'For Godsake Declan. What are you playing at?'

'Me? Where's the full backs. I'm out narrowing the angle.'

'Godsake.'

At the back of the school playing-fields the jail wall was so high it created echoes. In the trees around the pitch starlings were making metallic noises with occasional swooping notes. It was getting dark. Because it wasn't a real match the boys wore their own kit – and just knew who was on which side.

'Next goal's the winner.'

The ball had bounced across the track and Declan hopped the fence and kicked it out from there. A voice said,

'Bloody eejit.' Declan looked round startled. There was nobody there. Only the B-Special on guard duty at the foot of the jail wall. 'You were too far out. You should never let anybody chip you like that.' It *was* the B-Special. In all his years at the school Declan had never heard one of these guys speaking. Yet they were always there, day and night, at the base of the thirty-foot grey brick wall. They'd worn a track in the grass pacing up and down. Declan looked over his shoulder.

'D'you say something?'

'Yeah. I said you were too far out.'

'Says who?'

'Says me.'

'And what would you know about it?'

'More than you think, sonny boy.'

They were separated by a distance of twenty or thirty feet. The B-Special was up on a low terracing of grass. It seemed a stupid distance to continue talking. Declan looked over his shoulder to check which end of the field the ball was.

'I used to be a talent scout,' said the B-Special.

'Aye, that'll be right.'

'Naw, seriously.'

'Who for?'

'A club across the water.'

'Bollicks.' Declan vaulted the two-stranded wire fence and ran into his goal. The cold was really getting to him now. He wanted to jump up and down, to slap his arms, but he was conscious of being watched. He didn't want to look foolish, jumping about like a kid for no reason. Lights came on in the top row of windows in the jail – the Republican wing.

One night they had heard the prisoners from there shouting and rattling metal things against their windows. Tin mugs, it had sounded like. That was bad. Thinking about them in there. But what was worse was knowing the prisoners could hear *them* – playing football – shouting when they scored –

arguing about whose throw-in it was. People were really annoying about these things – throw-ins and corner kicks. This was what carried into the jail. Bickering. People who could go home for their tea or walk down the street or do anything they liked – people who were free – arguing and bickering.

A guy in a Celtic shirt led a charge out of the gloom and connected with a shot. Declan leapt and got his fingertips to it, deflecting it for a corner. Somebody slapped him on the back as he lay in the mud.

'Saved, wee man.'

What if the guy *was* a talent scout? Had he seen that? The corner was taken and the ball cleared.

After a while there was a bit of shouting and a ragged cheer at the other end.

'Is that it?' Declan called but nobody paid any attention to him. The boys began to move away. He could hear the twang of wire and the scuffling of boots on the cinder track as they made their way down to the classroom where they changed.

'Thanks for telling me,' he shouted at them. Still they ignored him. He ran back to the goalposts to collect his cap with his money rolled in it.

'Hey, c'mere.' Declan looked up. It was the B-Special again.

'What?'

'I said c'mere.'

Declan scissor-stepped over the wire fence and paused at the foot of the embankment. The B-Special said,

'I wanna ask you something.'

Declan waited.

'Come up here.'

Declan looked round. The others had disappeared. Away in the distance a light came on in the Nissan hut classroom. He dug his studs into the grassy slope and moved up a bit.

'I'm not gonna bite you.'

Declan shrugged in the darkness.

'The thing I wanna ask you is – that's a Roman Catholic school, right? Well answer me this. There's Roman Catholic priests in there, right? I see them walking round the track.'

Declan nodded, still waiting for the question.

'D'you smoke?'

'Yeah.'

The B-Special reached into his pocket. The material of his raincoat sleeve made a kind of whistling noise as it slid against itself. Declan could see the pale cigarettes sticking out of the packet offered to him in the darkness. His hands were dirty but the mud had almost dried. He reached over and took one. There was a metallic clunk and a Zippo lighter flamed.

'Maybe I'll keep it for later,' Declan said.

'You'll fuckin smoke it now.' Declan didn't know whether the man was joking or not. He lit Declan's cigarette and one for himself. In the light from the Zippo Declan saw that the man had a thin black moustache. He looked far too young.

'My question is this – these Roman Catholic priests – what do they do for sex?'

'They don't do anything. They're celibate.'

'What age are you, son?'

44

'Sixteen.'

'If you believe that you'll believe anything.'

'I am. I'll be seventeen in March.'

'Naw – I mean the celibate item.'

'They don't get married or anything.'

'It's the anything part I wanna hear about.'

'They give themselves to God. To being good.'

'And those black dresses they wear – '

'Soutanes.'

'Whatever you call them . . . All them buttons – walking round the track with their hands behind their backs. Or in their pockets, more like. Are you trying to tell me those guys do nothing. And they have equipment the same as the rest of us.'

'Yeah – as far as I know.'

'You're gullible, son. Dead gullible. They're a crowd of fuckin hypocrites. Liars.'

There was a long silence. Declan inhaled the smoke and put his head back and blew it out as if he was in the confined space of a toilet cubicle. He would have to stay here and finish the cigarette. The Dean or somebody might be hanging around the changing rooms. He had been caught twice – in the Dean's words – 'engaging in his habit'. And caned both times. 'You, of all people, should know that it stunts your growth.'

'Liars and hypocrites,' said the B-Special again.

'They are not.'

'How do you know?'

'I know some priests and maybe . . .'

'Maybe what?'

'I'm maybe going to . . . be one.'

'What – a priest?' The B-Special laughed, a low kind of chuckle. 'Fuck me.' He shook his head from side to side. 'I'm always putting my foot right in it.' He cleared his throat. 'I find that very sad. A waste – because you were shaping up as all right of a lad to me. What's your name?'

'Declan.'

'Declan what?'

'Declan MacEntaggart.'

The B-Special laughed, this time out loud, and said,

'You'd better be a priest because you'll not get too many jobs with a name like that. Are you a boarder or a day-boy?'

'A boarder.'

'From where?'

'Ardboe.'

'Fucksake. Where's that?'

'Lough Neagh – near Cookstown.'

'That's Republican territory up there. Crowd of rough men, by all accounts.'

'Where are you from?'

'Glengormley.' The B-Special unslung his gun and set it barrel up against the foot of the wall. He then hunkered down to smoke his cigarette. His head was now almost on a level with Declan's. 'See this,' he said, nodding at the wall. 'You get bored out of your fuckin mind at this.'

'You weren't scouting for any team.'

'Only taking the piss. I wanted you to make a couple of good saves. I was bored outa my mind up here.'

Declan felt spits of rain on his bare legs. The few saves he had made earlier had covered his haunch and side in black wet muck. Goalmouth cinders left fine scores of blood on his knees. He tried to get to the end of his cigarette. He took several quick puffs at it so that it became hot and soft.

'You're rushing that,' said the B-Special. He straightened up from his crouched position.

'It's freezin. I gotta go. The rain's starting.' Declan tossed the lit cigarette on the grass and squashed it with the studs of his boot.

'When are you going to give me that back?'

'What?'

'The fag.'

'You're taking the piss again.'

'I'm not fuckin made of money. You owe me one, kid. I'll be here tomorrow afternoon again. Same time.' The B-Special finished his cigarette and spun it away into darkness.

'I can't.'

'Why not?'

'The whole school is on silent retreat tomorrow.'

'Silent retreat? What in the name of God's that?'

'A day when people don't talk. They pray.'

'Sounds like an army. Tip-toeing. Backwards.' He laughed and so did Declan.

'How can I give you back your fag – if I don't even know who you are – or what you look like?'

The B-Special changed his position and suddenly a bright torch shone in Declan's eyes. The B-Special turned it on

47

himself, lighting up his face from below. Declan could barely see because his eyes were recovering from the sudden glare. Bright spits of rain crossed its beam.

'That's me,' said the B-Special. 'Special Constable Irvine Todd.' He looked about nineteen but was probably older. He had one of those young faces – so young that he tried to age it with a moustache.

'Maybe see you,' said Declan and danced down the slope sideways. He shook some coins from his cap and pulled it tightly on his head. The B-Special shouted after him.

'Hey!' Declan turned. The torch beam wobbled across the high wall. 'This never happened.'

'What?'

'You and me – talking. It's against the rules, fuck them. Okay?'

'Fair enough,' said Declan. Constable Irvine Todd was shining his torch at the wall, wiggling it, gliding the bright circle away from him until it became a bright ellipse then plucking it back again.

'Bloody eejit,' said Declan. He was now over the wire and running towards the light of the changing rooms.

When it began to get dark Declan headed for the track. A flock of starlings swooped over the jail wall and condensed as it changed direction. There were only one or two boys walking round – on their own because of the silence. A uniformed guard was standing at the foot of the jail wall, partly hidden by bushes. Declan walked past him once, trying to see if it was

Special Constable Irvine Todd. This guy wore the peak of his hat pulled down low on his face and was at such a distance he could have been anybody. If Declan climbed the fence and sneaked up and it wasn't the one he knew the guy might shoot him. B-men had a reputation for being trigger-happy. The starlings settled in the trees at the far side of the track and began chattering. Declan waited and stared up at the B-Special.

'Hey!' It felt ridiculous because Declan spoke the word instead of shouting it. The B-Special turned his head.

'It's you again.'

'Yeah.'

'I'm dying for a smoke, son.'

Declan looked all round then stepped over the wire. He was screened from the track now by the bushes.

'The excitement up here's been fierce. My nerves is jangling. Three murders and a rape and ten breakouts.' Declan put his hand in his pocket and produced the cigarettes. A white packet of Senior Service. 'Jesus, where do you get the packets of five?'

'The day-boys go down for us. I told him ten but he musta been deaf.' Todd produced his Zippo lighter and took a cigarette from the packet.

'Whatcha mean the dayboys go down for you?'

'We can't. We're not allowed out.' Declan slid the flap closed.

'Why not?'

Declan shrugged. 'School rules – boarders' rules.'

'They don't trust apprentice priests?'

'Not all of us are going on for the priesthood.'

'Fuck that for a lark.' Declan was putting the thin packet back in his pocket. 'Are you not having one yourself?'

'Naw – ' Declan looked over his shoulder. 'I've gotta go.'

'For fucksake. I'll look a right prick standing here smoking on my own.'

'It's a bit risky.'

'Have a cigarette, big lad. If anybody objects I'll blow their legs off.' He slapped his gun with the flat of his hand. 'Come on.' He flicked the lighter and held it out to Declan. In the wind the flame fluttered blue within the metal guard. Declan took out the packet again and got a cigarette. He hurried to light it.

'Thanks.' He cupped the cigarette in the palm of his hand and nodded at the gun. 'What is it, anyway?'

'A gun.' Declan smiled. The B-Special said, 'A nine millimetre Sten. They make the handles outa paper clips.'

'It's like your lighter. All those holes in the barrel.'

'You might as well have a fucking spear. No accuracy. You just can't keep it down.' He imitated firing the gun from his waist. 'Dju-dju-dju-dju – a figure of eight pattern. No matter how hard you try you can't keep it down – it goes all over the fuckin place.'

'I know nothing about guns,' said Declan. He felt safer crouching down. The B-Special leaned against the jail wall.

'What did you say you were doing today?'

'A silent retreat.'

'That's it.' The B-Special snapped his fingers. 'I was trying to

50

remember the name for my Ma. A silent retreat. I couldn't remember.'

'Were you talking to your . . . mother about . . . ?'

'Aye, last night. I says "Ma, you'll never believe it but I was talking to somebody who's going to be a Roman Catholic priest." I like to tease her. It drives her round the bend. She's a fierce oul bigot.' He shook his head and laughed. 'Tell me this – what's the point? What good's it going to do anybody?'

'What?'

'Silence. Not speaking?'

There was a pause.

'It allows you to listen to what God is saying to you.'

'You didn't think *that* one up yourself.' Todd stared at him. 'That's Roman Catholic priest talk, if ever I heard it.' Declan didn't answer. 'And what did he – with a capital aitch – say to you today?'

'This is not a subject to joke about. It's private.'

'Point taken – it's like sex. What's your name again?'

'Declan.'

'Tell me this, Declan, do you intend to get your hole, before you become a priest?'

'Don't be so bloody filthy.' Declan straightened up from his crouching position with the intention of going. The cigarette was too big to throw away and he couldn't walk down onto the track with it. He looked at it between his fingers.

'Okay, okay. Stay where you are. I like to take the piss now and again. But you're beginning to sound a bit like my Ma.'

'Naw, really. I better be going.'

'Getting on your high horse, eh? Grammar School boy tells one of Her Majesty's Special Constables to get stuffed.'

'It's not that. I don't like filth.'

'Like what?'

Declan shrugged.

'Sex things . . . things like that are just . . .'

'It's the world, son. You'd better get to know it if you're gonna spend the rest of your life tidying it up. You better know what happens beneath the blankets – every fuckin push and pull of it – before you go telling people what they're not allowed to do.'

'Shakespeare didn't have to murder somebody before he wrote "Macbeth".'

'You're trying to blind me with science now.' Declan looked down at his feet, trying not to laugh. The worn patches of his black leather shoes had gone pale with walking through the wet grass. 'You've got to know the ins and outs of everything.' The B-Special paused. 'Do you know there's a brave bit of rummaging goes on down by the handball alleys.'

'Rummaging?'

'Boys rummaging in each other's trousers.'

'You're making that up.'

'Swear to God. I can see it all from up here. Queer as fuck – these boarding schools.'

'Look, I shouldn't be here.'

'And I shouldn't be talking to you. But I am, ampta?'

The lights came on in the Republican wing of the jail. Declan threw his cigarette into the grass.

'I'd better go.'

'Do you have any friends in there?'

'Where?'

The B-Special nodded to the lit windows.

'No.'

'Are you a Republican?'

'I'd like to see a United Ireland, if that's . . .'

'How could you have a United Ireland with you and me in it?' He laughed out loud and punched the air. 'Fuck the Pope and No Surrender.' Declan smiled at the slogans. 'Nahhh – you're too nice a young lad to be friends with that scum. Sometimes I think this wall's here to stop people breaking in and lynching the bastards. Here – have another.' The B-Special held out a packet of ten Gallagher's Blues. Declan refused.

'Two in a row makes me dizzy.'

'You're the first Roman Catholic I've ever talked to – apart from one guy in work.'

'Work?'

'Aye, this caper is only part-time. In the mornings I do a milk round – white coat in the mornings, black at night. The money's no great shakes but it's better than nothing. If the milk round paid more I wouldn't have to be standing here like some kind of a fuckin doo-lally talking to you.'

'Thanks a lot.'

'But there's advantages – barmen are shit scared of us. A couple of us go into a pub in uniform and the drink's all free – and as much as you can smoke. Here.' He held out his packet of cigarettes again. Declan hesitated. 'Are you too good for my brand? I suppose you'd smoke them if they were Gallagher's Greens.'

'Naw – naw it's not that.'

'At least it's a packet of ten.'

Declan took a cigarette and was about to light it when he heard something down on the track. He paused and stared into the darkness.

'Wait.' The B-Special clunked the lid of the Zippo back into place putting out the flame. He said,

'Who is it?'

'I dunno.'

The figures came closer, their feet impacting on the cinder track. Declan could now hear their voices, then he recognised the deep laugh.

'It's the Dean,' he said, crouching down. He heard the other voice indistinctly, but enough to know who it was.

'So what?'

'Shh . . .'

'What's wrong?' said the B-Special. Declan shushed him again. The B-Special's voice changed to a whisper. 'Christ boy, you're really afraid of these guys.' He hunkered down beside where Declan was crouching and slapped the metal of the Sten with his open hand. 'Do you want me to cut them in half with this?' Declan shook his head and put a warning finger to his lips. The walking priests were right below them now. Declan imagined he could see their white collars at the same height in the dark. Their voices were low and he could not make out what they were saying. They passed and Declan stood up again. The B-Special whispered,

'Which one's the Dean?'

'The nearest.'

'And the other one?'

'Father Cairns – teaches Latin. He's okay.'

'No Jesuit's okay.'

'They're not Jesuits.'

'They're all fuckin Jesuits as far as I'm concerned.'

'You don't listen.'

The B-Special leaned forward and spun a spark from the Zippo wheel with his thumb.

'You don't really believe in God, do you?'

Declan lit his cigarette and breathed out the smoke. 'I do. Very much so.' He looked after the priests on the track. He could hear them faintly but he could no longer see them. He cleared his throat and said, 'The world is a very complex place. Right?'

'Aye, one-way streets . . . singing . . .' The B-Special paused and thought. 'And fuckin glass lampshades with dead flies in them. My Ma hates that.'

'Well, something as complex as the world just couldn't happen. There must be a supreme intelligence behind it. Right?' The B-Special nodded in an exaggerated fashion, mocking Declan's seriousness. Declan ignored him.

'How many times would you have to take all the bits of a watch and throw them up in the air before they'd land and start telling the time?'

'A hell of a lot. One hell of a lot.'

'So . . .'

'So what?'

The argument as he remembered it being outlined in Canon Sheehan's *Apologetics* had seemed simple. He hesitated.

'I mean if the world is as complex as a watch – which you have just agreed – then a watchmaker – aye ee – God, or some intelligence called God, had to put it together.'

'That is SO FUCKIN STUPID I can hardly believe you said it, Declan. The most complicated thing I know is my fuckin milk round. Who made that up? God? It just happened. People who drink milk live in different places. It's as simple as that.'

'I think you're being purposefully stupid.'

'Oh you do, do you?'

'Yes.'

'The world is not complex. It's dead fuckin simple. A stone is a stone. And a wall is a wall.' He slapped the wall with the flat of his hand.' And this wall is full of fuckin stones. Am I right? Is that complex or simple?'

'There's no point,' said Declan. He began backing down the slope.

'You're so like a Roman Catholic priest, Declan – I think you'll be one.'

'I hope so.'

'I think you'll go the whole hog and become a Jesuit.'

'I'm away back now.'

'Why would anyone want to be a Roman Catholic priest? It's SO totally fuckin perverse – God gave you a dick TO USE.'

'You're being filthy again.'

'No – I'm serious.'

'You don't understand.'

'I certainly do not. I need to have certain items explained to me.'

'God gave us appetites. By abstaining – by denying ourselves things we become stronger people. Going off sweets in Lent, kinda thing. Discipline. It doesn't mean to say there's anything wrong with sweets.'

'Why don't you abstain from learning then, from studying. Why don't you stay stupid – like me? That'd be a great sacrifice. For fucksake, who do you think you're kidding? I left school at fourteen and it was the wisest move I ever made.'

'I think you've an inferiority complex.'

'Huh! Listen to him. Listen to the second-class citizen,' said the B-Special. 'I suppose you want me to be an A-Special.'

'There's no such thing,' said Declan.

'There fuckin IS. Was. In the twenties. They were needed to keep you bastards getting too big for your boots.' He stabbed his forefinger at Declan's face. 'What age did you tell me you were, son?'

'Seventeen next month.'

'Well, stop fuckin patting me on the head. You have that Papish tone in your voice.'

'You're far too touchy. I wasn't meaning any of that.'

'So – I'm far too touchy – eh?' He thought for a moment then raised the Sten gun and swung it slowly round until the muzzle pointed at the boy. 'I'm a man with an inferiority complex?' The bones of Declan's chest felt as if they were about to cave in. He said,

'I don't know much about guns but I know that's definitely not allowed.'

'I never was one for the rules, was I, Declan?' He was using the gun like a rifle, sighting along the barrel at Declan's heart. They stood like that for what seemed a long time. Declan was afraid that he was going to faint. He kept swallowing.

'You're being really stupid . . .' Declan heard his own voice shaking.

'That's because I haven't had a great education . . .' Declan found the power to move and began to edge down the slope. 'Stay where you are and finish your cigarette.' The boy hesitated.

'Stop pointing that thing at me.'

'I'm giving the orders. Say your prayers. Yes – yes what a good idea. Say after me – Our father WHICH art in heaven . . .'

Declan backed down the slope staring at the gun. It was almost pitch dark now. He flung what remained of the cigarette away and stepped over the wire onto the track. He wanted to run but he walked as casually as he could. The B-Special shouted after him,

'Education nowadays isn't worth a tup-ney fuck. I'm glad I left when I did.'

Declan didn't look over his shoulder but he felt the gun pointing at the middle of his back and the sensation burned there all the time he was walking towards the lights of the school. It seemed to take ages before he had the courage to turn.

Even in the dark, the whiteness of his face must have been visible at a distance. From the base of the wall the B-Special shouted at the top of his echoing voice,

'Fuck the future.'

LOOKING OUT THE WINDOW – I

Your man gradually became aware of his tongue when he caught a cold for the third time that winter. Now he stood mouth-breathing, staring out the window, waiting for his wife to come back with the shopping.

It was too big. He was sure it was swollen. It used to sit snugly but now, at this minute, he felt it had risen like yeast-bread. With each breath it dried out a little more. His lips were cracked and dry but he could worry about them another time.

He went to the bathroom and put his tongue out at the shaving mirror. There was no furring. This was a favourite of his mother's – the coated tongue. It meant you deserved a good clearing out. He made a point of the tip of his tongue and turned it up to examine the strings underneath. There were certain bits of people, he thought, which didn't stand up to scrutiny.

He turned away from the mirror and allowed the tongue to slot back in its place. It still felt too large. Or did it? It was being conscious of it that worried him – its every movement, touching his teeth, rubbing against the edges of a molar, tracing the ridges on the roof of his mouth. He let it relax and tried to forget about it.

He walked across the hall and went into the front room to continue his mouth-breathing. He stood at the window looking down the street, clinking the few coins he had in his pocket. Not so much clinking but rubbing the milled edges together with a little metallic sawing noise.

AT THE BEACH

They sat opposite each other across the table in the small apartment. He was just out of bed. The first thing he had done was to peer through the slats of the shutters at the view – white apartments, two cranes and, beyond, the blue of the Mediterranean. He wore underpants and a shirt to cover his stomach. She had risen earlier to go to the Supermercado for some essentials. The *Welcome-pack* was only meant to get them through the night – tea-bags, some sachets of coffee, a packet of plain biscuits.

'The price of cereal would frighten you,' she said. He nodded, trying to open the cardboard milk carton. 'I'm not exactly sure what it is in pounds or pesetas but that packet of All-Bran costs the same as a bottle of brandy.'

'It's worth it for the bowels. The bowels will thank me before the week's out.' He tried to press back the winged flaps of the waxed carton but they bent and he couldn't get it open. 'Fuck this.' He stood up and raked noisily through the drawer of provided cutlery for a pair of scissors. She was looking in the cupboards under the sink.

'Hey – a toaster.' She held it up. He smiled at its strange design – it was as if someone had removed the internal workings of an ordinary toaster. She plugged it in to see if it would work and the wires glowed red almost immediately. The socket was beneath the sink so the toaster could only sit on the floor. 'Stamped with the skull and cross-bones of the Spanish Safety Mark.' She put on two slices of bread.

'Is this goats' milk?' He made a face but persevered spooning the All-Bran into his mouth.

'I didn't get you a paper – they only had yesterday's. And we read yesterday's on the plane.'

'We want a holiday from all that.' He reached down and brushed an ant off his bare foot. 'Did you sleep?'

'It was getting light through the shutters,' she said. 'The crickets went on all night. They're so bloody loud.'

'What's it like outside?'

'Hot – and it'll get worse as the day goes on. The Supermarket has . . .' She laughed. 'I was going to say central heating but I mean . . .' She wobbled her hand above her head.

'Air conditioning.'

'Yeah – you come out onto the street and feel that hot wind – like somebody left a hair-dryer on. The Supermarket's a Spar, would you believe. I thought they only existed in Ireland. And I got Irish butter – here in Spain.'

He killed an ant on the table with his thumb.

'These wee bastards are everywhere.' He bent forward and stared down at the maroon tiled floor. 'Look – Maureen.'

'The toast.' She hunkered down and turned the bread just as it was beginning to smoke.

*

When they had eaten breakfast they made love and after a while he said, 'I love you,' and when her breath had come back she said,

'Snap.' She reached out and touched the side of his face. 'I mean it, Jimmy,' she said and smiled, hugging him to herself. Their faces were close enough to know they were both smiling.

In the plane Maureen had bought a long-distance Fly-Travel kit which contained light slippers and a neck pillow. It also included some stickers which said *Wake for Meals*. Jimmy stuck one on his forehead and pretended to be asleep. Maureen laughed when she saw it.

'It's what life's all about,' he said. He put on his salesman's voice. 'Have you seen our other bestselling sticker, sir? *We give birth astride the grave.*'

'Wake for meals.' Maureen said it aloud again and laughed. 'Let me have a shower – then we'll find out where this pleasure beach is.'

He laughed and said, 'We *know* where it is.'

They followed the signs which said *Playa*. His hands were joined behind his back, she carried a bag with the camera and the towels and stuff. They stopped on the hill overlooking the beach to study which part of it would suit them best. The place was crowded and colourful.

Sun-beds were stacked at intervals. When they got down they took one each and camped near the beach bar. Jimmy sat on his like a sofa while Maureen stepped out of her dress. She had her bathing suit on. She stood putting sun cream on her shoulders and legs.

'Do my back,' she said, handing him the bottle. She lay on her front on the sun-bed. He squeezed some cream into the palm of his hand and began to rub it into her skin. He looked around him. Most of the women were bare-breasted. Everyone seemed to be tanned. Mediterranean people with jet-black hair and dark olive eyes.

'We're pale as lard,' Jimmy said.

'Only for a day or two. Who cares anyway – nobody knows us here.'

'I care,' he said – then after a pause, 'Nipples the colour of mahogany.'

'What?'

'Never mind.'

'Act your age, Jimmy. They're young enough to be your daughters.'

'I can look, can't I? Anyway, who's talking about girls – the boys have nipples, too.'

When he finished doing her back he did his own arms and legs. He opened his shirt and saw the pallidness of his own skin. If anything, it was whiter than Maureen's.

'Don't forget the top of your feet and . . . your bald spot.'

'I meant to buy a fucking hat.' When he had his body covered with cream he joined his hands and rubbed the top of his head with his moist palms as if he was stretching. Then he lay down on his back. That way his gut was less noticeable.

'Do you miss the girls?' Maureen said.

'Like hell. It's about bloody time we got away by ourselves.' He laughed and said, 'It's like it used to be. Just you and me, baby.'

'It's different now.' Even though her eyes were closed she made an eye-shade cupping her hand over her brow. 'Maybe better.'

'God it's hot.'

'That's what we paid all the money for.'

'Did you remember to put the butter back in the fridge?' Maureen nodded.

'I hate butter when it's slime.'

'I hate *anything* when it's slime.'

'This place makes me so . . .' Jimmy looked around at the people sprawled near him. If they were reading books he could tell by the authors whether or not they were English-speaking. Jilly Cooper, Catherine Cookson, Elizabeth Jane Howard. Others who just lay there sunbathing gave no clue. So he lowered his voice. 'It makes me so fucking randy.'

A couple in their early twenties came up and kicked off their sandals. They dropped all their paraphernalia on the sand and began to undress. Jimmy watched the girl, who was wearing a flimsy beach dress of bright material like a sarong. Beneath she wore a one-piece black swimsuit. The lad pulled off his T-shirt. He was brown with a stomach as lean as a washboard. He said something to his girlfriend and she replied, laughing. They sounded German or Austrian. The girl elbowed her way out of the shoulder straps of her bathing suit and rolled it down, baring her breasts. She continued rolling until the one-piece was like the bottom half of a bikini. They both sat down and the girl took a tube from her basket. She squirted a teaspoonful of white cream onto her midriff and began rubbing it up and over her breasts. They lifted and fell as her hand moved over them. She looked up in Jimmy's direction and he quickly turned his head towards Maureen.

'What?' said Maureen, sensing his movement.

'Nothing.' He shook his head.

About mid-day Jimmy put his shirt on and they went up to the patio of the beach bar for a drink and something to eat. They sat in the shelter of a sun umbrella looking over the beach. The luminous shadow cast by the red material of the umbrella made them look a slightly better colour. Maureen leaned towards him and said,

'Don't look now but I hear Irish voices.'

'Jesus – where?' Jimmy, with his elbows on the table, arched both hands over his brows and pretended to hide.

'Behind me and to the left.'

Jimmy looked over her shoulder. There were three men around a table smoking. They all were wearing shirts and shorts. One of them had a heavy black moustache. Maureen was about to say something when Jimmy shushed her. He listened hard through the foreign talk and rattle of dishes. He heard some flat vowels – but they could have been Dutch or Scottish. American even.

'I'm not sure,' said Jimmy.

'Well, I am.'

'Let's steer well clear.'

A waiter approached their table.

'Try your Spanish,' said Maureen.

'Naw – it's embarrassing.' But when the waiter opened his pad Jimmy said, 'Dos cervezas, por favor.'

'Grande o pequeño?'

Jimmy cleared his throat.

'Uno grande y uno pequeño,' he said.

'That's one large and one small, sir.'

Jimmy nodded. 'Gracias.'

'De nada.' The waiter disappeared indoors to the restaurant. Jimmy raised his eyebrows in a show-off manner.

'Not bad at all,' said Maureen. 'I hate all the th's – like everybody's got a lisp.'

When the beers came they toasted each other. Every time he raised his glass an ice-cold drip would fall down the open front of his shirt onto his belly and startle him. He cursed – thought there was a crack in the glass or the beer mat was wet.

'They put the stupid fuckin beer mat round the stem instead of underneath.' Maureen pointed out to him it was condensation. The beer was cold – the air was hot – condensation formed on the outside of the glass – each time he picked it up it would drip on him. The beer mat round the stem was a none too successful attempt to prevent this.

'You're too smart for your own good,' he said.

Maureen looked up at the menu displayed on the wall.

'We'll have to eat a paella some night.'

'Yeah – seafood.'

'It's a kind of enforced intimacy. They only do it for two people.'

'No paella for spinsters.'

'Or priests.'

'If it was in Ireland they'd make it for *his Riverence* and throw the half of it out.'

They both smiled at the thought. There was a long silence between them. Jimmy shifted his white plastic chair closer to hers. His voice dropped to a whisper.

'Who – I don't know whether I should ask this or not . . .'

'What?'

'Naw . . .'

'Go on.'

'Who was the first man you ever did it with?' She stared at him. 'You don't have to tell me – if you don't want to.'

'I don't want to and it's none of your business.' She spoke quietly and without anger.

'Can you remember the first time you had an orgasm? I mean – not even with somebody. By yourself, even.'

'Not really. All that early stuff is smudged together.'

'Come on,' he whispered. 'That's one of those questions like where were you when they shot Kennedy. Everybody knows. The first time that happens to you it's like being in an earthquake or something. You *remember*. It's like your first kiss . . .'

She hesitated and screwed her face up. 'It might have been the back of a car . . .' He leaned forward to hear her better. 'This is nonsense. Why do you want to know?'

'We've been married twenty-five years. We should have no privacy – no secrets from one another.'

'This is just stirring up poison.' She looked away from him at the sea. There were pedalos and wind surfers criss-crossing the bay.

'I just want to know.'

'It's like picking scabs on your knee. No good'll come of it.' She finished her beer and stood up. 'I'm going for a swim.'

When she had gone Jimmy sat staring at the white table top. He raised one finger at the waiter and said,

'La cuenta, por favor.'

They swam and dried off, then reapplied the sun cream. They did each other's back.

'It was a bit nippy getting in at first,' said Maureen. 'I didn't expect that. But it was lovely when you got down.'

The German or Austrian couple had gone off. Jimmy picked them out from the other bathers. They were playing knee-deep in the waves with a velcro ball and bats which fitted onto the hand. If the ball touched the glove even lightly it stuck fast.

Maureen settled down on her front, crossing her arms as a pillow for her cheek. She sighed.

'This is *so* nice. I deserve it.'

'I'm sorry about that – that before the swim – up at the bar. But sometimes – there's a thing in me that . . . wants to *know* about you before I met you. There's a part of me that's jealous of the time when I didn't know you.'

'Jimmy . . .'

'What?'

'You're starting again.'

'Sorry.'

'Where do you think the girls are? Right now,' said Maureen.

'God knows. Half way across the Nevada desert. New Orleans? L.A.? I just hope they don't hitch. Them hitching makes me nervous. Bloody lorry-drivers.'

'They'll be fine.'

The German couple came up the beach, laughing, their hair sleeked and wet. The boy dropped the bat and ball game beside Maureen. The girl rolled down her bathing suit again and lay down on her back just a few feet from Jimmy. She was breathless. Her wet stomach rose and fell as she gasped for breath. Jimmy stared at her. Gradually over a minute or so her breathing became normal. She turned to get the sun on her back and her breasts appeared columnar before she eased herself down.

'How does that work?' Maureen asked.

'What?'

'That bat and ball game.'

'Velcro.'

'Oh . . .'

'Two materials – one has hooks, the other loops. When they hit they stick.'

'I've only seen it used as a zip.'

'It was one of those ideas that came from nature. The burr sticking to the animal hair.'

'Clever balls.'

'I've just expanded your world for you, Maureen. You should be grateful.'

To avoid the risk of sunburn they went back to the apartment at three o'clock. They walked slowly through the heat.

'I feel utterly drained,' said Maureen. There was a flight of steps to where their apartment was and they both paused half way up.

'It's the heat,' said Jimmy and they both smiled at each other. He leaned against the wall which was in shadow. The stones forming the wall were round and porous.

'They build everything here out of Rice Crispies.'

A lizard suddenly appeared on the sunlit side of the wall. 'Behind you Maureen.' She looked and stood still. It had come to a halt in an S-shape. It was bright green. With a flicker of movement it was gone as suddenly as it had appeared.

'Wasn't it lovely to see that?' said Maureen. 'I've never seen one before. They move so fast.'

'They're cold-blooded, that's why they seem so energetic in this heat. It's like us going for a run on a frosty morning.'

'I feel my world expanding all the time.'

The shutters were closed and the place was dark. They had a shower together and Maureen got to choose the luke-warm temperature of the water. Then they made love again.

'We'll not be able to stick the pace', said Jimmy, ' – without the kids.'

'Today is lovely but I don't want you – y'know – every time we close that door. We need our own space.' She was boiling the kettle for a coffee and it seemed to take ages. The room was still dark but slivers of the harsh hot light and white buildings could be seen through the top slats of the shutters. Jimmy sat in his white towelling dressing-gown looking down at the table. The ant population had increased since the morning.

'They're after our toast crumbs,' he said. They seemed to be forming a line to and from the table, clustering round a crumb or an almond flake from a biscuit. There were too many now to start killing them.

'Just let them be,' said Maureen. 'It's not as if they bite.'

Jimmy was following the line to its source. Down the table leg and across the kitchen floor to the jamb of the bathroom door. There was a millimetre gap between the wood and the tiles and ants were disappearing into it. Others were coming out.

'There must be a nest somewhere.'

'Or a hill,' said Maureen.

'Maybe they've been on this route for ten million years,' he said. 'Somebody just built this place in their way fifty years ago. This is their track – why should they change just because some bastard of a developer puts a house in their way.'

She poured two coffees and set one on the table for him. She side-stepped the shifting black line of ants and said,

'They do no harm to anybody.'

He decided to watch one – it seemed sure of itself heading away from the table with news of food. It came face to face with others and seemed to kiss, swerve, carry on. Away from the main line there were outriders exploring – wandering aimlessly while in the main line the ants moved like blood cells in a vein.

'There's no point in killing one or two. The whole thing is the organism. It would be like trying to murder somebody cell by cell.'

'Just let them be.'

'The almond crumbs are yours,' he said but still he flicked ants from his bare feet whenever he felt them there.

The next day they went to the beach and sat in the same place. Jimmy looked around and saw that Jilly Cooper, Catherine Cookson and Elizabeth Jane Howard were just behind him.

'We're all creatures of habit,' he said. 'It's as bad as the fucking staff room.' The mid-day sun made the sand hot to the touch. Maureen had moved from Factor Fifteen and was putting on Factor Six. He did her back for her and she lay down.

'We agreed not to talk about things like that.'

'Okay – okay.'

'Until we get back.'

They lay there roasting for about thirty minutes, Maureen flat out, Jimmy resting on his elbows taking in the view. He had bought a white floppy hat with little or no brim and a pair of sun-glasses in the Supermercado. The glasses gave him greater freedom to look around without noticeably moving his head.

'The Germans are absent,' he said, 'and no note.'

'Which Germans?'

'The Velcro Germans.'

'I didn't realise they were Germans. What is the Assistant Head's particular interest there?'

'Nothing. They just haven't turned up.'

'Liar.'

'The girl is a class act – a bit magnificent.'

Maureen laughed and rubbed a little cream onto her nose with her little finger.

'Do you fancy a walk?' she said.

'Yeah sure.' He put on his shirt and let it hang out over his shorts and they walked to the rocky cliff at the far end of the beach. People here were brown and mostly Spanish-speaking. There was a lot of laughing and shouting.

'It seems to be compulsory not to listen. People all speak at the same time.'

'That's because you don't have the faintest idea what they're saying. Two people from Derry would sound just the same – if you didn't know – if your English . . .'

'They just seem to interrupt each other all the time.'

They swam off the rocks and the water seemed warmer than the previous day. As they walked back across the beach Jimmy took Maureen's hand. They nudged up against each other and fleetingly she put her head against his shoulder.

'This is *so* good,' she said. 'I like Public Displays of Affection – no matter what you say.'

'Why does it matter when nobody knows us?'

'I know us,' she said. 'Sometimes you can be so bloody parochial.'

In the middle of the afternoon the German couple arrived and sat down about three feet to the left of the spot where they had been the day before. From behind his sunglasses Jimmy watched the girl undress. Today she wore the bottom half of a white bikini. He heard the boy use her name. *Heidrun*, he called her. Jimmy tried to nod hello to her but she didn't notice. She shook out, then spread a large towel, adjusting and flattening the corners. All her attention was taken up with her friend.

'They might as well be on a deserted beach in Donegal,' said Jimmy, nodding at the couple. Heidrun knelt down on the spread towel and her boyfriend leaned over and nuzzled into her neck. They both lay down face to face, their feet pointing in Jimmy's direction.

'They'd be covered in goose-pimples,' said Maureen. Jimmy stared at the gusset of the white bikini facing him. It was as if the closeness of the German couple had some influence on them and Jimmy and Maureen moved closer together. He whispered in her ear.

'Why is it that the only woman on the beach who seems to have any pubic hair is you?'

'You mean you go around looking?'

'A man cannot help but notice these things.'

'You mean a Catholic repressed man. A lecher. A man with a problem.'

'You lie there like some kind of a farmer's wife from the backabeyond or . . . or somebody from Moscow.'

'I meant to do it before I came away – but with the rush and all . . . It's not that obvious – is it?' She looked down at herself.

'Not really but . . .'

'Anyway, who's looking at me in that tone of voice – at my age. Catch yourself on, Jimmy. Go and buy me an ice cream.'

He got to his feet and put on his shirt. 'What flavour?'

'The green one with the bits of chocolate in it.'

'What's it called?'

'Jesus, you can point, can't you?'

He fiddled in her purse for pesetas, then went off towards the bar.

At the bar he noticed again the three suspected Irishmen from the first day. They sat beside the counter. Jimmy listened as he pointed out and bought the ice-cream. Maureen was right again. They were definitely from the North of Ireland. They were talking about football. Something about Manchester United and the English league. Two of them wore tartan shirts, the third a T-shirt with Guinness advertising on it.

When he got back to Maureen he gave her the ice-cream.

'I saw your friends up there. I think they're RUC men.'

She licked the peppermint green and crunched a bit of the chocolate.

'What makes you think that?'

'I dunno. They look like Chief Constables or Inspectors. I feel sorry for them. If you were a policeman in the North where would *you* go for your holidays?'

She didn't answer. She nodded towards the German couple.

'There's been plenty of PDA since you left.' She smiled and winked at Jimmy. The couple were lying with their faces an inch apart staring into each other's eyes. Occasionally the boy would trail the back of his knuckles down her naked side. Maureen beckoned Jimmy's ear to her mouth.

'Meine Liebe,' she whispered.

That evening on the patio of *Nino's* they decided to have the seafood paella for two. They had been given complimentary glasses of a local sherry and Jimmy asked to have the order repeated. He would pay for them. As he suspected, when the waitress brought the drinks she said, 'On the house.'

Jimmy drank Maureen's second drink as well as his own two.

When the waiter brought the double paella he showed it to them. They both nodded in appreciation at its presentation. It was served from a much-used, blackened pan and the waiter made sure to divide everything equally. Three open navy blue mussel shells to one plate, three to the other. One red langoustine to you and one to you.

Maureen hated it – wet sloppy rice with too much salt and the most inaccessible parts of shellfish. Things that had to be broken open and scraped, recognisable creatures which had to have them backs snapped and their contents sucked. At one point Maureen raised her eyes and gave a warning to Jimmy. The three Northern Ireland men were sitting down at the next but one table from them. She scrutinised them.

'I'm sure they're not policemen.' They were directly behind Jimmy and he had to twist in his chair to see them. One of them caught his eye and recognised him from the beach. They nodded politely to each other.

'They're like people out of a uniform of some kind,' said Jimmy. 'Maybe they're screws – from Long Kesh.'

'Or security men.'

Maureen gave up on the paella.

'How do you tell a lie in Spanish – it was lovely but there was too much of it?' There was a lull in the noise of conversation and dish-rattling and Maureen heard a name float across from the next but one table. Jimmy said,

'If you are not willing to talk about your early sexual experiences – I am.'

'Not again.'

'In those days I was a vicious bastard – every time I went out with a woman I went straight for the conjugular.'

She laughed and said, 'You think I didn't notice.' She paused and looked at him. 'You made that up.'

'Of course I did. I just said it, didn't I?'

'No I mean you thought it up one day and then waited for a time when you could use it. Tonight's the night.'

He nodded vigorously, pouring himself another glass of wine. Maureen put her hand over the top of her own glass.

Another, different name came floating across from the Northern Ireland table. Maureen made a face as if something was just dawning on her.

'I know,' she said when she had swallowed the food in her mouth. 'They're priests. The first name I heard was Conor and now there's Malachy.'

'Catholic names don't make them priests.'

'But black socks do.'

'Keep your voice down. If we can hear them they can hear us.'

'Two of them's wearing black socks,' whispered Maureen. 'It all fits now. Why would three aging men go away on holiday together?'

'A homosexual ring?'

'They never go *on* the beach. They never take their clothes off. They are keeping an eye on each other. Since the Bishop of Galway nobody trusts anybody else.'

'One of them has a moustache.'

Maureen looked over his shoulder and checked.

'So?'

'I've never seen a priest with a moustache.'

'Maybe there's two of them priests and the one with the moustache is the priest's brother. You're right – the one with the moustache is wearing white towelling socks.' Jimmy checked under the table. Maureen smiled and said, 'There's nothing worse than a priest's brother. All the hang-ups and none of the courage.'

'Are they drinking?'

'Yes.'

'They probably *are* priests then.' They laughed at each other. Jimmy reached out and covered her hand with his. 'Would you like coffee or will we get another bottle?'

'Coffee is fine for me.'

'I'm sorry to go on about this – but there must have been no shortage of men *trying it on* before me.'

Maureen stared at him. 'What is this – where did all this shite suddenly come from, Jimmy?'

'I've just been thinking. Seeing things that remind me. You were a very attractive woman when we first met . . .'

'Gee thanks . . .'

'No I don't mean that. You still are. I'm saying – in comparison to others in the field.'

'In the field – you're making it sound like a cattle fair – have a good look at her teeth.'

'That's a horse fair you're thinking of.'

'Jimmy.' She stared hard at him. 'Teach me how to be right all the time?'

'It wouldn't work – two in the one family.'

'Then one of us would have to leave,' said Maureen. 'It's that time of life. Everybody is leaving everybody else. They stayed together for the kids. Now that's over.'

'You don't feel like that, do you?'

Maureen looked at him and smiled. She shook her head.

'Not yet.'

They walked back to the apartment across the dark beach. They both took off their shoes and walked ankle deep at the water's edge. It was warmer than during the day. There was a white moon reflected on the water. They held hands again until Jimmy stopped for a piss in the sea. Maureen walked on.

*

In the apartment Jimmy fell down onto the sofa.

'I'm going to have a drink of that duty-free whiskey before it's all drunk.'

'And who's liable to drink it?'

'Me.' He grinned and rose to pour himself one. She laughed at him.

'Have you drunk all *that* since we came here?'

'Lay off. I'm on my holidays too.'

'But we drink a bottle of wine – minus one glass for me – every night as well.'

'Over dinner.'

'That makes no difference.'

'Plus a few beers. Maureen, will you stop counting. And some of that Spanish fucking gin.'

'With no ice.'

'Ice is where the bugs get in.' He diluted his whiskey with bottled water *sin gas* he had bought for the purpose. 'Speaking of which . . .' He moved to the bathroom and looked down at the tiled floor.

'Holy shit! Maureen will you take a look at this.' He hunkered down and sipped his whiskey.

'Oh my God,' said Maureen. What had been a trickle of ants was now a torrent – a stream that was moving both ways. From the chink in the bathroom tile they moved across the floor in a bristling stream to the table leg, up the table leg onto the table – into the cereal packets. The stream divided and part of it went to the rubbish bin where they had thrown their leftovers – melon rinds, tea-bags, stale bread.

'It's fizzin with them,' said Maureen, lifting a bread wrapper from the bin between her finger and thumb. 'Are they just a fact of life. Will we have to put up with them all the time we're here?'

'As long as they're not in the bed,' said Jimmy. As he stood up some of his whiskey slopped over. The ants panicked, began moving faster. The stream parted and moved around the droplets of whiskey, ignoring it. 'Why don't they get pissed?'

'Maybe they will do – after work,' said Maureen.

'They're really prehistoric, aren't they. And so *silent*. In the movies there would be a soundtrack.'

Maureen made tea with a tea-bag in a mug and they went out onto the small balcony. There was a candle in a bottle left by a previous tenant and Maureen lit it and set it on the white plastic table. Jimmy sipped his whiskey and put his feet up on the balcony rail.

'I just love being in my shirt-sleeves at this time of night. Can you imagine what it's like at home?' Maureen sighed a kind of agreement. The moon was low in the sky and criss-crossed by the struts of two cranes. Had the moon not been there the cranes would have been invisible. Jimmy nodded towards the candle.

'Somebody from the north. Remember that holiday in Norway?' Maureen nodded. 'Candles everywhere. The kids loved it. Flames burning *outside* restaurants. Never pulling their curtains – you could follow people moving from room to room.'

'You certainly did.'

'The bills – light shining out of everywhere. Here it's the opposite. Shutters – keep the light out. It's impossible to get the slightest glimpse inside a Spanish or an Italian house.' Jimmy sipped his whiskey and held it in his mouth for a while, savouring it. It was a thing he knew annoyed her. They didn't speak again for some time.

'You *really* don't like to talk about this stuff, do you?'

'No,' she said.

'I just want to know what happened to you before I met you.'

'I've told you everything there is to know – chapter and verse. Everything about my home and school . . .'

'But not sexually. You never mention anything about that.' She sipped her mug of tea holding it with both hands – the way she would sip tea in the winter. 'I'm jealous of not knowing you then. Your school uniform. Your First Communion. I am jealous of all the time I was not with you.'

'That's a kind of adolescent – James Dean – kind of thing to say.'

'I am jealous of every single sexual act *in which I was not involved.*'

She looked at his face in the candle light and realised he was serious.

'Jimmy, why are you torturing yourself about this? Leave it alone. Why should all this come up now – after twenty-five years? Maybe you feel threatened. Now that you're out of shape and balding you feel threatened.'

'Fuck off.'

'I'm going to bed.' She got up and went the long way round the table so he wouldn't have to take his feet down off the balcony rail.

He heard her shut the latch on the bedroom door and the creak of the bed as she got into it. He poured himself another whiskey larger than the last because she was not there to see the size of it. He drank several more glasses equally large and listened to the crickets and the English voices that were continually passing in the street below.

When Maureen woke at 4 am he still had not come to bed. She found him in the chair, his head tilted back, his mouth open and slanting in his face.

'Are you okay, Jimmy?' She put her arm beneath his and got him to his feet. He was mumbling something about 'those fucking priests' as she eased him down onto the bed and started to take his shoes off.

He was sick the next day and, although he tried to hide the fact by going out of the room, Maureen could hear the crinkling of him in the bathroom pressing indigestion tablets out of their tinfoil pack. When she accused him of drinking foolishly he blamed the paella.

'You've never done that in your life before, Jimmy. Not to my knowledge.'

'Got a bit pissed?'

'No – passed out – sitting in your seat.'

'I fell asleep, for fucksake.'

'I'm going to get you one of those wee stickers printed which says *Wake for Drinks*.' Maureen went to the fridge to put away the butter.

'Oh my God,' she said, 'would you look at this?'

'What?'

'There's ants crawling up the rubber seal of the fridge door.'

'We'll have to do something.'

In the coolness of the Supermercado Maureen, with the help of a small Spanish dictionary, made herself understood to the man she liked at the checkout. She wanted to kill ants. The man nodded, went off down between the aisles and came back with an orange-coloured tube.

'You have children?' he asked.

'Yes – two girls.'

He made a face which said – oh well, I don't think this is a good idea. He pointed at the black skull and crossbones on the side of the tube. Maureen realised what he meant and laughed at herself.

'My children are not here. They are big. Away.' He smiled and raised an eyebrow which Maureen interpreted as – you don't look old enough to have grown-up children. It was soft soap but she still liked him.

'Where ants come in.' He directed the nozzle downwards. Maureen nodded that she understood.

When she got back Jimmy was lying on the sofa still looking hung-over. She handed the tube to him and he insisted on looking up the instructions and ingredients in the dictionary.

'Jesus – it seems to be honey and arsenic.'

'The guy says you have to put it down where they're coming in.'

Jimmy heaved himself off the sofa and squatted down by the bathroom door. The stream of ants was now so dense that they blackened the floor in an inch-wide band. Millions coming, millions going. He unscrewed the lid and aimed the oily liquid into the crack they were pouring in and out of.

'Try this for size, my little ones.' Several drops fell on the tiles of the bathroom floor. Jimmy stood up and washed his hands thoroughly. Maureen came to see the effect the stuff was having.

'They are going daft, Jimmy. They're all lining up to drink it. Look at them.' The ants were now streaming in all directions but the main movement was to line up along the edge of the liquid. 'They can't leave it alone. Look they're dying.' The ones on the margin of the poison had ceased to move. Others nudged them aside to get at it. Maureen looked at the tile where the single drops had fallen. Ants had gathered round the edge of the drop and ceased to move.

'They're like eyelashes round an eye,' said Maureen.

'Christ – it's very dramatic stuff.' Jimmy looked down at the floor still drying his hands. 'Goodnight Vienna.'

Maureen went out to go to the beach. If Jimmy felt better he would join her later. She had to pass the Supermercado so she stepped inside and gave the thumbs up to the guy at the checkout about the efficiency of the ant stuff. He nodded his head and smiled.

It was on the way down the hill that it occurred to her that maybe he didn't know what she'd been referring to. She became embarrassed at the thought. Maybe he didn't even know who she was – a man like him would smile at all his customers.

It was nice to be on her own. She felt good about herself. Her tan was beginning to be evident without being red. The pale stripe beneath her watch-strap acted as a kind of indicator. She was in no hurry to get to the beach and walked towards the old town looking in shop windows. She did not want to buy anything – just to look. Most of the shops were closed and she realised that it was *siesta*. The streets were empty. It was eerie – like in a movie after the bomb had been dropped. The flat stones of the pavement were hot and shining and she got the notion that she would slip on them if she was not careful. Pasted to a wall were posters for a fiesta which coincided with their last night. There were to be fireworks starting at 11 pm in the square at the harbour front.

She was now moving through an area of the town where she hadn't been before. The façade of a church appeared as she came round a corner. It seemed to grow out of a terrace of houses and looked very old and very Spanish. She walked along the street towards it. She was not knowledgeable about these things but she guessed it was mediaeval. In the curved arch above the door white doves blew out their chests and made cooing, bubbling noises. The main door was huge and ancient – studded with iron nails, each shaped like a pyramid. There was a smaller door cut into it. She tried the handle but found it locked. Now that she was excluded she wanted to see the inside more than ever. Several yards to the left of the main door was another side door. She was unsure whether it belonged to the next house or the church. She tried the handle and it swung open.

'Ah . . .' She stepped in. It wasn't really inside the church but in a colonnade alongside. At this end it was dark and cool but the far end was brilliant with sunshine. In between the colonnade of columns, arches of shadow sliced onto the walkway. She had a memory of looking out from a dark wood into sunlight. The door closed behind her with a rattle as the catch clicked. There appeared to be no way into the church from here. She walked down the colonnade towards the sunshine, listening to the slight itching sound the soles of her shoes made with the sandstone floor. The arches were curved, held up by pillars of blond stone which got lighter and lighter as they neared the source of the sunlight. Was she sufficiently dressed to go into the church? Her white T-shirt left her arms bare, but nobody could object to her Bermuda-length shorts. She felt slightly nervous – like a child expecting to be scolded for trespassing or intruding where she had no right to be. What if some *Monsignor* were to turn the corner and begin shouting at her in Spanish, yelling at her that this was the Holy of Holies. She paused and thought of going back. But she was so curious to see what lay beyond the source of the light. She walked hesitantly down the arcade and came upon a small square. It took her breath. There was something about it which made her love it with an intensity she had rarely experienced. There was no fear now of being caught. In some way she felt she had the right to be here. It was a square or atrium made of the same blond stone as the columns which formed the cloisters around its perimeter. In the centre was what looked like a font set up on a dais of steps. It had a spindly canopy of wrought iron. Maureen moved near the font and turned slowly to look around her with her head tilted back, looking up. Windows, three sets in each wall, overlooked the small courtyard but there appeared to be no one living behind them. There were no shutters, no curtains. Empty rooms. The sun was almost directly overhead. When she sat down on the steps the stone was warm. She was aware of the absolute silence – aware that outside this cloister was the quietness of a town in *siesta*. Inside, everything was intensified. Suddenly the silence was broken by the clattering of wings as several white doves flew onto the tiled roof. Maureen stood up and climbed the steps to the font. She leaned her elbows on the rim and looked at the round hole or shaft in the middle of it. She gave a little jump and leaned on her forearms, her feet off the ground, and looked down into the shaft. There was a white disc at the bottom.

'It's a well.' She unslung her bag from her shoulder and found a 25 peseta coin – the one with a hole in it – and dropped it down. Nothing happened and she was amazed at the silence.

How could there be nothing? Where was the sound of the coin dropping into the water below –

spluck!

She couldn't believe the depth. She took another coin and dropped it and counted as if making an exposure. A thousand and one – silence – a thousand and two – silence – a thousand and three – still silence – a thou –

spluck!

She heaved herself up again and looked into the well. The disc of light at the bottom rippled. There was something so *right* about this place. It was affecting her body. Her knees began to tremble. She held tight to the well head. She had to sit down on the steps and lean her back against the font.

She sat for the best part of an hour, sunbathing and absorbing the place. Occasionally she changed her position on the steps or walked in and out of the shadow of the cloisters. The place emphasised her aloneness. It felt as if it had been made for her and she should share it with no one. The cloister was a well for light – the cloister was a well for water. The word *Omphalos* came into her head. She connected the word to a poem of Heaney's she'd read somewhere. The stone that marked the centre of the world. The navel.

The sunlight and the clarity of the air squeezed into such a small space by the surrounding roofs became a lens which made her see herself with more precision. She did not think of herself as a middle-aged woman – she was still the same person she had been all her life – a child being bathed by her own mother – a teenager kissing. She was the same bride, the same mother-to-be in white socks and stirrups on the delivery table. Her soul was the same as that younger girl. She *felt* the same.

Soul was a word. What did it mean? People talked of stripping away layers to reveal the soul. It was not buried deep within her. It wasn't like that at all. Her soul was herself – it was the way she treated other people, it was the love for her children, for the people around her and for people she had never seen but felt responsible for. Her soul was the way she treated the world – ants and all.

She smiled at herself. In this place she knew who she was. In the hour she'd been here it had become sacred. She would remember this haven – this cloister – for the rest of her life.

By the time she got to the beach Jimmy was already there. He was lying flat out on a sun-bed with his back to the sun. Maureen went up and nudged his elbow with her shin.

'Hi.'

'Buenos días,' he said. He looked up sideways at her. 'Where have you been?'

'Around. I went up into the old town.'

'See anything?'

'The shops were closed. So was the church. Siesta.'

'What kept you?'

'Exploring. I had a coffee. Sat in an old courtyard for a while.'

It was too late in the day to get the value out of lying on a sun-bed so she began spreading a towel, having flapped it free of sand. 'Oh there's a fiesta tomorrow night – fireworks, specially for us leaving.'

'That's nice of them.'

'How are you feeling now?'

'Hunky dory.' But he groaned all the same when he was turning over to get the sun on his chest. He cradled the back of his head in his hands and from between his feet watched the German girl and her boyfriend. 'You missed it earlier on,' he said. 'I'm sure she was lying on his hand.'

'Jimmy – leave them alone. Don't be such a . . .'

'Remember that?'

'Sometimes I don't know what goes on in men's minds.' She took off her shorts and T-shirt and lay down on the carefully spread towel. The beach was noisy – an English crowd were shouting their heads off at the water's edge – there was a baby crying having its nappy changed – euro-pop played and dishes rattled constantly in the beach café. 'Or whether they've got minds at all.'

The next evening before they went out to eat they decided to try and get the whiskey 'used up' before going home. Because it was their last night they decided to dress up a bit. They sat on the balcony while it was still light. Maureen had a small whiskey and he a much bigger one.

'I better leave enough for a nightcap,' said Jimmy.

'But you'll be drinking all evening.'

'A nightcap's a nightcap. We judged the bottle well.'

'We?'

'Almost as well as the All-Bran. If we were to stay here a day longer the bowels would grind to a halt.'

They sat staring at the view – the sea straight at the horizon – the white buildings, the palm trees, the cranes.

'I'm going to miss this,' said Maureen. All that week they had seen no-one working on the unfinished apartments. The cranes were unmanned but they moved imperceptibly – at no time did they respond like a weather vane to the wind but whenever Maureen or Jimmy had occasion to look up the cranes would be in different positions and at different angles to each other.

'The recession must be hitting here too,' said Jimmy.

'It's back to normal next week.'

'Don't mention it – don't ruin our last night.'

'I think – I've been thinking . . . now that the kids are practically gone I might try and get a job.'

'Doing what?'

She shrugged.

'I might train for something.'

'At your age?' said Jimmy. 'No chance.'

'Why do you always put me down?'

'I'm just being *realistic*, Maureen.'

'I got three distinctions in A levels. I held a good job in the photo works up until you came along.'

'They were the days of black and white.' He laughed.

'They were the days when they sacked you for being pregnant.'

He finished his whiskey and stood.

'We'd better go if we want to eat *and* firework. Do I look okay?'

'Yeah, fine.' She picked a few grey hairs off the collar of his navy blazer and dusted away some dandruff.

'You look good,' he said and kissed her.

During the meal in the restaurant Jimmy drank three-quarters of the bottle of wine. He dismissed white wine as not drinking at all – 'imbibing for young girls', he called it. By the time they'd had their coffee Jimmy had finished the bottle. Maureen noticed that he was looking over her shoulder more than usual during the meal. She glanced round and saw an attractive, tanned girl in a white dress sitting by herself.

'She's lovely, isn't she?' said Jimmy.

Maureen nodded. 'Why's she by herself?'

'Because her lover has just gone to the crapper.'

'And there was me building a romantic story . . .'

'Do you want the rest of your wine?'

Maureen shook her head. He poured what was left of her glass into his.

'Get the bill, Jimmy.' He put his arm in the air and attracted the attention of the waiter. Left alone again he said,

'A woman by herself is the most erotic thought a man can have.'

'What d'you mean?'

'By herself she is the complete item. The brain, the body, the emotions. In the shower, in bed. Uninterfered with. Herself.'

'I still don't understand.'

'Sexy. Absorbed. Unreachable. Aloof. Detached.'

'I thought sexy was the opposite of detached.'

'A woman in a shop', said Jimmy, 'by herself is absorbed – choosing something to wear – looking through a rack of dresses.'

'Or even studying a book – or even *writing* a book.'

'You're really fucking bolshie this evening.'

The partner of the woman in white returned to the table.

'He's back,' said Jimmy. Maureen twisted in her seat to see.

'They can't be married,' she said. 'She smiled at him. That's very early days. Second or third date.'

'Remember that?'

She smiled and put her hand on his.

'I do,' said Maureen. 'Vividly.'

'That was a time of finding out . . . of knowing everything there is to know . . . There must be no privacy between people in love.'

'Crap Jimmy. You're talking the impossible. Anyway, there can never be a situation where you know *everything* about another person. It's harder to know one thing *for sure*.'

'Maybe.'

'When there's nothing left to know there's no mystery. We would all be so utterly predictable.'

The waiter brought the bill and they paid and left. Maureen checked her watch and saw there were only a couple of minutes before the fireworks were due to start. They walked quickly towards the main square.

*

It was a large open area overlooking the harbour. At the back of the square were the dark shapes of civic buildings. Gardens and pavements and steps descended to the sea. There were trees of different varieties symmetrically spaced. Looped between the trees were what looked like fairy lights but they were not working. Jimmy pointed them out to Maureen and laughed.

'They're about as organised as the Irish,' he said. 'If they had a microphone it'd whine.'

The square was filled with local people waiting for the fireworks. Amongst them, holidaymakers like Jimmy and Maureen were obvious.

Suddenly there was a whoosh of a rocket followed by an ear-shattering bang. Both Maureen and Jimmy jumped visibly. There was a sound of drums and the raucous piping noise of a shawm and ten or so figures pranced into the middle of the square.

'It's the fucking Ku-Klax-Klan,' said Jimmy.

They were dressed in white overalls, some like sheets, some like rough suits. Their heads were hidden in triangular hoods with eye-slits. Two or three of them were whacking drums, all of them were dancing – leaping and cart-wheeling.

'I don't like the look of these guys.'

'They're really spooky.'

'Like drunk ghosts.'

'They're more like your man – Miro,' said Maureen. The figures danced and dervished around, whirling hand-held fireworks and scattering fire crackers amongst the crowd who screamed and jostled out of their way.

'Jumpin jinnies, we used to call those,' shouted Maureen. The troupe of dancers pushed sculptures on wheels with fireworks attached – shapes of crescent moons, of angular trees, of whirling globes – from which rockets and Roman candles burst red and green and yellow over the heads of the public. Between the feet of the bystanders crackers exploded. The air was filled with screams of both adults and children as they leapt away from them.

'Jesus – this is so dangerous,' said Jimmy. 'They're breaking every regulation in the book.' The drums pounded and the pipe screeched on. As the sculptures were swung round they gushed sparks – sometimes it looked as if the sculptures moved *because* of the sparks – jet-propelled.

'Those robes must be fire-proofed. This wouldn't be allowed at home. It scares the shit outa me – All-Bran or no All-Bran.'

'It's so utterly primitive – prehistoric,' said Maureen.

'How could it be prehistoric. Gunpowder was invented in the middle ages.'

'There would have been an equivalent – fire, torches, sparks.'

'Come on let's get outa here before somebody gets hurt.' The troupe had split up and before Jimmy and Maureen could move three dancers had run up the steps and appeared behind them. Close up their robes were embroidered with Miro-like symbols. One of them held aloft a thing that looked like the spokes of an umbrella. Suddenly it burst into roaring fire – five Catherine wheels with whistles on them spraying sparks in every direction. They rained down on the crowd – white magnesium sparks – drenching them in light and danger and everyone screamed and covered their heads with their hands.

'Fucking hell,' shouted Jimmy. Maureen saw the white hot sparks bouncing off the cobblestones like dashing rain – white, intense, like welder's sparks. She tried to cover her head – she knew the skin of her shoulders was bare. But she felt nothing. Neither did Jimmy. They ran, Jimmy elbowing his way through the crowd away from the dancers, pulling Maureen after him by the hand. On the edge of the crowd they looked at each other and laughed.

'They're like kids' hand-held fireworks,' said Jimmy. 'They're harmless. Fuckin sparklers.'

'Are you sure?'

'I'm not going back to check, I'll tell you that.'

Again there was a series of enormous explosions just above their heads so that Maureen screamed out. What Jimmy had thought were broken fairy lights were fire crackers going off a few feet above their heads. They both ran holding hands.

They stopped at a small pavement area outside a bistro still in sight of the fireworks and they were both given a free sherry. The three supposed priests sat at a table near the door. They nodded recognition to each other. Jimmy ordered Menorcan gin and because he was going home the next evening allowed the barman to fill the glass with ice. They sat at the same side of the table, shoulder to shoulder, at a safe distance from the fireworks.

'It's pure street theatre,' said Maureen. 'The audience are involved because of their fear. The adrenalin flows. The costumes, the music, the fire – '

'It could never happen at home.'

'Yeah, we kill people outright.'

'The danger brings pleasure. It involves the audience totally.'

'Look,' said Jimmy. The young German couple were walking away from the fireworks. They had an arm around each other. They stopped to kiss and the boy slid both his hands down onto Heidrun's backside to hold her closer.

'They make a fine couple – even though we don't know their language.' When the kiss was finished the lovers walked passed the bistro. The boy's hand was worming its way down the back of her shorts and Heidrun was leaning her blonde head against his shoulder.

Jimmy mimicked the gesture and laid his head on Maureen's bare shoulder.

'I'd still be interested to know how far you went with previous – the men before me? You knew some pretty good tricks.'

She looked at him tight-lipped then moved away from his head.

'I wouldn't like to see you with another man *now* – but I'd like to have seen you with one *then*.'

'This got us nowhere before,' she said quietly. 'Jimmy, give it a rest.'

'No, why should I? Tell me about the first time you came, then.'

'I would if I could – if it's SO important to you. But I can't so I won't. Would you like to ask your daughters this question the next time you see them?'

'Don't be stupid. That's a totally different thing.'

'I don't see why.'

'Why can't you tell me?' said Jimmy. 'You're repressed. Why can't we talk openly about this?'

'It's *you* that's repressed,' she almost shouted, 'wanting to know stuff like that. It's becoming a fixation.'

'It was a question I'd always wanted to ask. I thought – what better time. Holiday. Alone. No kids.'

'No time is a good time for questions like that.'

When she lifted her sherry her hand was shaking.

'Don't make such a big thing of it.'

'When you do those kind of things with people there's a pact – a kind of unspoken thing – that it's private – that it's just between the two of you. Secrecy is a matter of honour.'

'So you *have* done it.'

'No – *don't be so stupid* – it could be just kissing or affection or kidding on or flirting. Whatever it was it's none of your fucking business.'

She did not finish her sherry but got to her feet.

'I'm going home. You can stay here with your priests, if you like.'

*

At about three o'clock Jimmy crawled into bed beside her and wakened her from a deep sleep. He was drunk and crying and apologising and patting her shoulder and telling her how good she was and how much she meant to him and that he would never ever ever ever leave her. He was a pest but that's the way he was and she could like it or lump it. But she was a wonderful woman.

'Jimmy, shut up – will you?' Now that he had disturbed her she got up and went to the bathroom. When she came back he was snoring loudly. She closed the latch of the bedroom door so that he wouldn't waken and tried to get some sleep on the sofa. She felt alone on the narrow rectangle of foam – lonely even – a very different feeling to the wonderful solitariness she had experienced in the cloisters. She couldn't sleep. The thought of leaving Jimmy came into her head but it seemed so impossibly difficult, not part of any reality. Nothing bad enough had happened – or good enough – to force her to examine the possibility seriously. Where would she live? How could she tell the girls? What would she tell her parents? Jimmy was right about getting a job. It seemed so much simpler to stay as they were. The status quo. People stayed together because it was the best arrangement. She slept eventually and in the morning she could not distinguish when her deliberations had tailed off and turned to dreaming.

'Jimmy, I think we should try and salvage something from the last day.' She spoke to wake him. Startled, he turned in the bed to face the room. Maureen had the large suitcase open on the floor. She was holding one of his jackets beneath her chin then folding the arms across the chest. She packed it into the case, then reached for another. Jimmy tried not to groan. He sat on the side of the bed and slowly realised he was still in his clothes. She must have taken his shoes off him. He put his bald head in his hands.

'Is the kettle boiled?'

'It was – a couple of hours ago.'

He got up and finished the packet of All-Bran – bran dust at this stage. He made tea and a piece of toast in the skeletal toaster. Maureen continued to pack.

'What time's the flight?' he asked.

'Eighteen hundred hours.'

'I hate those fucking times. What time is that?'

'Minus twelve. Six o'clock.'

Jimmy had a shower and changed his clothes. After he cleaned his teeth he packed everything in sight into his wash-bag. He came out of the bathroom with a towel round his middle. He was grinning. Maureen was kneeling on the floor packing dirty washing into a Spar plastic bag.

'I've got the hang-over horn.'

'Well, that's just too bad. There's things to be done.'

'Indeed there are.'

Maureen got a brush and a plastic dust-pan. The living room floor was scritchy with sand spilled from their shoes. Earlier in the week Jimmy had knocked over a tumbler and it had exploded on the tiled floor into a million tiny fragments.

She thought she had swept them all up at the time but still she was finding dangerous shards in the dust.

Between the bathroom and the living room the dead ants still blackened the margins of the honey-poison. There was no mop and she had not wanted to sweep them up and make the floor sticky underfoot. Now it didn't seem to matter and she swept the whole mess onto the dust pan. Individual ants had lost their form and were now just black specks. She turned on the tap and washed them down the plug hole.

Jimmy was sent down the street to the waste-bins while she put any usable food in the fridge as a gift for whoever cleaned up. When he came back everything was done and the cases were sitting in the middle of the floor. Maureen was drinking a last coffee and there was one on the table for him.

He stood behind her chair and put his arms round her.

'I'm sorry,' he said. 'About last night. Going on and on about those . . .' He kissed the top of her hair.

'Jimmy – promise me. You mustn't annoy me about that again.'

'Okay – scout's honour.' He began massaging the muscles which joined her neck and shoulders.

'Oh – easy – that hurts.'

'What time do we have to vacate this place?'

'Mid-day.'

He bent over and whispered, 'That gives us twenty minutes.'

They left their luggage at the Tour company headquarters for the remaining hours and went down to the beach. They walked along to the rocky promontory at the far side.

'I've really enjoyed this,' said Jimmy. 'The whole thing.'

'Who did you meet up with last night?'

'They said they were social workers. Which means they admitted to being priests in mufti. They were okay.'

'What did you talk about?'

'I'm afraid eh . . . Large chunks of it are missing. We seemed to laugh a lot. I think they were every bit as pissed as I was.'

'I don't like the look of them. They're the kind of people who'd go out of their way to take a short cut.'

They sat on the rocks watching the sea swell in and out at their feet.

'It's very clear,' said Jimmy. The water was blue-green, transparent.

'You can be a real pest when you come in like that. You look so *stupid*.'

'Sorry.'

They became aware of an old couple in bathing suits paddling into the sea close by the rocks. They looked like they were in their eighties. The woman wore a pink bathing cap which was shaped like a conical shell. Her wrinkled back was covered in moles or age spots as if someone had thrown a handful of wet sand at her back. The old man had the stub of an unlit cigar clamped in the corner of his mouth. Their skin was sallow. Mediterranean but paler than those around them for not having been exposed to the sun – although their faces and arms were the nut-brown colour of people who had worked in the open. The old man was taking the woman by the elbow and speaking loudly to her in Spanish, scolding her almost. But maybe she was deaf or could not hear, her ears being covered by the puce conical cap. She was shaking her head, her features cross. They were thigh-deep and wading. When the water rose to her waist she began to make small stirring motions with her hands as if she were performing the breast stroke. She made the sign of the cross. The old man shouted at her again. She dismissed him with a wave of her hand, then submerged herself by crouching down. She kept her face out of the water. The old man reached out from where he stood and cupped his hand under her chin. She began to make the breast-stroke motions with her arms, this time *in* the water. The old man shouted encouragement to her. She swam about ten or twelve strokes unaided until she swallowed sea water, coughed and threshed to her feet. The old man yelled and flung his damp cigar stub out to sea.

'Jesus – he's teaching her to swim.' Jimmy turned and looked up at his wife. Maureen was somewhere between laughing and crying.

'That's magic,' she said. 'What a bloody magic thing to do.'

BY TRAIN

'. . . *your man was travelling from Glasgow to Aberdeen by train. In the opposite corner of the carriage sat a man pretending to be absorbed in his copy of the* Scotsman. *He did not speak until after they had pulled out of Dundee and then he had a strange, almost unbelievable tale to tell.*

' "*Recently,*" *he said,* "*I was travelling from Perth to Lancaster and my only carriage companion was a young woman. Even though she wore a veil of some kind I could see that her features were of great beauty. But what fascinated me most was her hands. She wore gloves for much of the journey but shortly after we had pulled out of Kilmarnock she removed them to reveal scars the like of which I have never witnessed. She must have seen my eyes flinch away because she said, 'I hope, sir, I do not offend you but behind these broken hands is a story which some people find hard to believe. Recently I was travelling by train between Lancaster and Wolverhampton and the compartment was occupied by just one other person. He was of average height, a thick-set man in his forties, dressed in the garb of a country gentleman. He did not speak to me,' she said, 'but shortly after pulling out of Crewe he burst into tears. His whole body was convulsed with weeping. I offered him my handkerchief from my sleeve.* "You are most kind," *he said through his sobs.* "Forgive me." "There is nothing to forgive," *I replied.* "Sometimes we are asked to endure things too heavy for the human heart," *he said.* "Up until Tuesday last I was married to a girl of unsurpassable beauty twenty years my junior. On our honeymoon we were travelling by train from Berlin to Venice. In our carriage were two German farmers, each with a muzzled goose on his knee . . ." ' " '

THE WAKE HOUSE

At three o'clock Mrs McQuillan raised a slat of the venetian blind and looked at the house across the street.

'Seems fairly quiet now,' she said. Dermot went on reading the paper. 'Get dressed son and come over with me.'

'Do I have to?'

'It's not much to ask.'

'If I was working I couldn't.'

'But you're not — more's the pity.'

She was rubbing foundation into her face, cocking her head this way and that at the mirror in the alcove. Then she brushed her white hair back from her ears.

'Dermot.'

Dermot threw the paper onto the sofa and went stamping upstairs.

'And shave,' his mother called after him.

He raked through his drawer and found a black tie someone had lent him to wear at his father's funeral. It had been washed and ironed so many times that it had lost its central axis. He tried to tie it but as always it ended up off-centre.

After he had changed into his good suit he remembered the shaving and went to the bathroom.

When he went downstairs she was sitting on the edge of the sofa wearing her Sunday coat and hat. She stood up and looked at him.

'It's getting very scruffy,' she said, 'like an accordion at the knees.' Standing on her tip-toes she picked a thread off his shoulder.

'Look, why are we doing this?' said Dermot. She didn't answer him but pointed to a dab of shaving cream on his earlobe. Dermot removed it with his finger and thumb.

'Respect. Respect for the dead,' she said.

'You'd no respect for him when he was alive.'

She went out to the kitchen and got the bag for the shoe things and set it in front of him. Dermot sighed and opened the drawstring mouth. Without taking his shoes off he put on polish using the small brush.

'Eff the Pope and No Surrender.'

'Don't use that word,' she said. 'Not even in fun.'

'I didn't use it. I said eff, didn't I?'

'I should hope so. Anyway it's not for him, it's for her. She came over here when your father died.'

'Aye, but he didn't. Bobby was probably in the pub preparing to come home and keep us awake half the night.'

'He wasn't that bad.'

'He wasn't that good either. Every Friday in life. Eff the Pope and NO Surrender.' Dermot grinned and his mother smiled.

'Come on,' she said. Dermot scrubbed hard at his shoes with the polishing-off brush then stuck it and the bristles of the smaller one face to face and dropped them in the bag. His mother took a pair of rosary beads out of her coat pocket and hung them on the Sacred Heart lamp beneath the picture.

'I'd hate to pull them out by mistake.'

Together they went across the street.

'I've never set foot in this house in my life before,' she whispered, 'so we'll not stay long.'

After years of watching through the window, Mrs McQuillan knew that the bell didn't work. She flapped the letter-box and it seemed too loud. Not respectful. Young Cecil Blair opened the door and invited them in. Dermot awkwardly shook his hand, not knowing what to say.

'Sorry eh . . .'

Cecil nodded his head in a tight-lipped way and led them into the crowded living-room. Mrs Blair in black sat puff-eyed by the fire. Dermot's mother went over to her and didn't exactly shake hands but held one hand for a moment.

'I'm very sorry to hear . . .' she said. Mrs Blair gave a tight-lipped nod very like her son's and said,

'Get Mrs McQuillan a cup of tea.'

Cecil went into the kitchen. A young man sitting beside the widow saw that Mrs McQuillan had no seat and made it his excuse to get up and leave. Mrs McQuillan sat down, thanking him. Cecil leaned out of the kitchen door and said to Dermot,

'What are you having?'

'A stout?'

Young Cecil disappeared.

'It's a sad, sad time for you,' said Mrs McQuillan to the widow. 'I've gone through it myself.' Mrs Blair sighed and looked down at the floor. Her face was pale and her forehead lined. It looked as if tears could spring to her eyes again at any minute.

The tea, when it came, was tepid and milky but Mrs McQuillan sipped it as if it was hot. She balanced the china cup and saucer on the upturned palm of her hand. Dermot leaned one shoulder against the wall and poured his bottle of stout badly, the creamy head welling up so quickly that he had to suck it to keep it from foaming onto the carpet.

On the wall beside him there was a small framed picture of the Queen when she was young. It had been there so long the sunlight had drained all the reds from the print and only the blues and yellows remained. The letter-box flapped on the front door and Cecil left Dermot standing on his own. There were loud voices in the hall – too loud for a wake house – then a new party came in – three of them, all middle-aged, wearing dark suits. In turn they shook hands with Mrs Blair and each said, 'Sorry for your trouble.' Their hands were red and chafed. Dermot knew them to be farmers from the next townland but not their names. Cecil asked them what they would like to drink. One of them said,

'We'll just stick with the whiskey.' The others agreed. Cecil poured them three tumblers.

'Water?'

'As it is. Our healths,' one of them said, half raising his glass. They all nodded and drank. Dermot heard one of them say,

'There'll be no drink where Bobby's gone.' The other two began to smile but stopped.

Dermot looked at his mother talking to the widow.

'It'll come to us all,' she said. 'This life's only a preparation.'

'Bobby wasn't much interested in preparing,' said the widow. 'But he was good at heart. You can't say better than that.' Everybody in the room nodded silently.

Someone offered Dermot another stout, which he took. He looked across at his mother but she didn't seem to notice. The two women had dropped their voices and were talking with their heads close together.

One of the farmers – a man with a porous nose who was standing in the kitchen doorway – spoke to Dermot.

'Did you know Bobby?'

Dermot shook his head. 'Not well. Just to see.' He had a vision of the same Bobby coming staggering up the street about a month ago and standing in front of his own gate searching each pocket in turn for a key. It was a July night and Dermot's bedroom window was open for air.

'I see your curtains moving, you bastards.' A step forward, a step back. A dismissive wave of the hand in the direction of the McQuillans'. Then very quietly,

'Fuck yis all.'

He stood for a long time, his legs agape. A step forward, a step back. Then he shouted at the top of his voice,

'Fuck the Pope and . . .'

Dermot let the curtains fall together again and lay down. But he couldn't sleep waiting for the No Surrender. After a while he had another look but the street was empty. No movement except for the slow flopping of the Union Jack in Bobby Blair's garden.

Cecil came across the room and set a soup-plate full of crisps on the hall table beside Dermot.

'Do you want to go up and see him?'

Dermot set his jaw and said,

'I'd prefer to remember him as he was.'

'Fair enough.'

The man with the porous nose shook his head in disbelief.

'He was a good friend to me. Got my son the job he's in at the minute.'

'Bully for him.'

A second farmer dipped his big fingers in the dish and crunched a mouthful of crisps. He swallowed and said to Dermot,

'How do you know the deceased?'

'I'm a neighbour. From across the street.'

'Is that so? He was one hell of a man. One hell of a man.' He leaned over to Dermot and whispered, 'C'mere. Have you any idea what he was like? ANY idea?'

Dermot shook his head. The farmer with the porous nose said,

'When Mandela got out he cried. Can you believe that? I was with him – I saw it. Big fuckin tears rolling down his cheeks. He was drunk, right enough, but the tears was real. I was in the pub with him all afternoon. It was on the TV and he shouts – what right have they, letting black bastards like that outa jail when this country's hoachin with fuckin IRA men?'

He laughed – a kind of cackle with phlegm – and Dermot smiled.

The signs that his mother wanted to go were becoming obvious. She sat upright on the chair, her voice became louder and she permitted herself a smile. She rebuttoned her coat and stood up. Dermot swilled off the rest of his stout and moved to join her on the way out. The widow Blair stood politely.

'Would you like to go up and see him, Mrs McQuillan?' she said.

'I'd be too upset,' she said. 'It'd bring it all back to me.' Mrs Blair nodded as if she understood. Cecil showed them out.

In their own hallway Mrs McQuillan hung up her coat and took an apron off a peg.

'Poor woman,' she said. 'Did they ask you to go up and see him?'

'Aye.'

'Did you go?' Her hands whirled behind her back tying the strings of the apron.

'Are you mad? Why would I want to see an oul drunk like Bobby Blair laid out?'

He went into the living room and began poking the fire. Their house and the Blairs' were exactly the same – mirror images of each other. His mother went into the kitchen and began peeling potatoes. By the speed at which she worked and the rattling noises she made Dermot knew there was something wrong. She came to the kitchen doorway with a white potato in her wet hands.

'You should have.'

'Should have what?'

'Gone up to see him.'

'Bobby Blair!' Dermot dropped the poker on the hearth and began throwing coal on the fire with tongs.

'Your father would have.'

'They asked *you* and you didn't.'

'It's different for a woman.'

She turned back to the sink and dropped the potato in the pot and began scraping another. She spoke out to him.

'Besides I meant what I said – about bringing it all back.'

Dermot turned on the transistor and found some pop music. His mother came to the door again drying her hands on her apron.

'That poor woman,' she said. 'It was bad enough having to live with Bobby.' She leaned against the door jamb for a long time. Dermot said nothing, pretending to listen to the radio. She shook her head and clicked her tongue.

'The both of us refusing . . .'

As they ate their dinner, clacking and scraping forks, she said,

'It looks that bad.'

'What?'

'The both of us.'

Dermot shrugged.

'What can we do about it?'

She cleaned potato off her knife onto her fork and put it in her mouth.

'You could go over again. Say to her.'

'What?'

'Whatever you like.'

'I don't believe this.'

She cleared away the plates and put them in the basin. He washed and she dried.

'For your father's sake,' she said. Dermot flung the last spoon onto the stainless steel draining-board and dried his hands on the dish towel, a thing he knew she hated.

He slammed the front door and stood for a moment. Then he walked across the street, his teeth clenched together, and flapped the letter-box. This time the door was opened by a man he didn't know. Dermot cleared his throat.

'I'd like to see Bobby,' he said. The man looked at him.

'Bobby's dead.'

'I know.'

The man stepped back then led the way into the hallway. The farmers were now standing at the foot of the stairs. The one with the porous nose was sitting on the bottom step swirling whiskey in his glass.

'Ah – it's the boy again,' he said. The man led the way up the stairs. Dermot excused himself and tried to slip past the sitting farmer. He felt a hand grab his ankle and he nearly fell. The grip was tight and painful. The farmer laughed.

'I'm only pulling your leg,' he said. Then he let go. It was like being released from a manacle. Somebody shouted out from the kitchen.

'A bit of order out there.'

In the bedroom the coffin was laid on the bed, creating its own depression in the white candlewick coverlet. The man stood back with his hands not joined but one holding the other by the wrist. Dermot tried to think of the best thing to do. In a Catholic house he would have knelt, blessed himself and pretended to say a prayer. He could have hidden behind his joined hands. Now he just stared – conscious of the stranger's eyes on the back of his neck. The dead man's face was the colour of a mushroom, his nostrils wide black triangles of different sizes. Fuck the Pope and No Surrender. Dermot held his wrist with his other hand and bowed his head. Below the rim of the coffin there was white scalloped paper like inside an expensive box of biscuits. The paper hid almost everything except Bobby's dead face. Instead of candles the room was full of flowers. The only light came through the drawn paper blinds.

From downstairs came the rattle of the letter-box and the man murmured something and went out. Left alone Dermot inched nearer the coffin. His father was the only dead person he had ever seen. He pulled the scalloped paper back and looked beneath it. Bobby was wearing a dark suit, a white shirt and tie. Where his lapels should have been was his Orange sash – the whole regalia. All dressed up and nowhere to go. Dermot looked up and saw a reflection of himself prying in the dressing-table mirror. He let the scalloped paper drop back into place. Footsteps approached on the stairs.

Two oldish women were shown in by the stranger. One was Mavis Stewart, the other one worked in the papershop. Mavis looked at the corpse and her lower lip trembled and she began to weep. The women stood between Dermot and the door. Tears ran down the woman's face and she snuffled wetly. The woman from the papershop held onto her and Mavis nuzzled into her shoulder. She kept repeating, 'Bobby, Bobby – who'll make us laugh now?' Dermot edged his way around the bed and stood waiting. The women took no notice. Mavis began to dry her tears with a lavender tissue.

'I never met a man like him for dancing. He would have danced the legs off you. And he got worse when the rock and roll came in.' Dermot coughed, hoping they would move and let him pass.

'And the twist,' said the woman from the papershop. 'I think that boy wants out.'

Mavis Stewart said,

'Sorry love,' and squeezed close to the bed to let him pass. Dermot nodded to the stranger beside the wardrobe.

'I'm off.'

'I'll show you out.' The stranger went downstairs with him and went to open the front door. Dermot hesitated.

'Maybe I'd better say hello to Mrs Blair. Let her see I've been up. Seeing Bobby.'

He knocked on the living-room door.

'Yes? Come on in.'

He opened it. Mrs Blair was still sitting by the fire. She was surrounded by the three farmers. Dermot said,

'I was just up seeing Mr Blair.'

'Very good, son. That was nice of you.' Then her face crumpled and she began to cry. The farmer with the porous nose put a hand on her arm and patted it. Dermot was going to wave but checked his arm in time. He backed into the hallway just as young Cecil appeared out of the kitchen. It was young Cecil who showed Dermot out.

'Thanks for coming,' he said. 'Again.'

A VISIT TO NORWAY

In Heathrow the girl at Security, feeding bag after bag through the X-ray machine, says to your man,

'May I ask what's in your cardboard tube, sir?'

'A reproduction of a woodcut – "The Kiss" – by Edvard Munch.'

'I much prefer his mezzotints,' says she, patting his chest, his thighs and buttocks.

IN BED

The buzzer sounded long and hard – a rasp which startled her even though she knew to expect it – maybe *because* she knew to expect it. She splayed her book on the carpet so as not to lose her place and went across the hall to her daughter's bedroom – moving quickly because the long buzz created a sense of urgency. The girl was crouched on the bed, her face turned towards the door in panic.

'Mum, another one,' she said and pointed to her hand pressed down hard on the pillow.

'Take it easy. Relax.' Her mother hurried out of the bedroom and came back with an empty pint glass from the kitchen.

'How can I relax with a thing like that in bed? It might breed, might be laying eggs.'

'Wait.'

'Dad uses a bar of soap. Don't let it get away.' The girl's face was anxious and much whiter than usual. She was wearing pyjama bottoms and a football shirt of red and white hoops. 'I hate them – I hate them.' Her voice was shaking. Her mother approached the pillow with the pint glass inverted.

'Easy now – lift your hand.'

The girl plucked her hand away. The black speck vanished – it was there, then, suddenly, it wasn't – before the glass could be slammed down. The girl screamed.

'It's jumped.'

'Blast.'

The girl held her hair back from her face, peering down at the surface of the sheet.

'It's gone – it's got away.'

'Aw no . . .'

'Oh I hate them, I really hate them.' The girl's voice was on the edge of tears. She was shuddering. 'They make me feel so . . . dirty.' Her mother bent over and stared closely at the surface of the white sheet, pulling it towards her a little to flatten a wrinkle.

'Don't move,' she whispered. The girl gave a little gasp.

'Where? Where is it?'

Her mother raised the glass and quickly pressed it down onto the sheet.

'Gotcha.'

The girl bent over and looked inside. She pulled up her lip in distaste when she saw the black speck.

'Eucchh.' It jumped again and she squealed even though it was inside the glass. 'I'm never going to let that cat in here again. I hate it.'

'Take over,' said her mother. 'Press it down tight. Don't let it out.'

She went out of the bedroom and her daughter heard her filling a basin with water. She pressed the glass down until her arm ached. The rim of the glass dug into the sheet and made the centre swell like a pin-cushion. The flea disappeared.

'Oh no. Mum!' She put her face down close. The black speck reappeared. Her mother came back, forced to take short steps with the weight in the plastic basin. Some of the water slopped over the sides and formed droplets on the carpet.

'Here,' she said. 'Let me at it.' She set the basin on the floor and looked around. She took a Get Well card from the mantelpiece and turned it over to the plain white side. Her daughter let go of the glass and the mother began to slide the card beneath it while still pressing down.

'Don't let it get away,' said the girl. She was holding her hair back with a hand on either side of her face. The black speck was flinging itself into the roof of the pint glass.

'Easy does it.' Her mother completed sliding the card all the way across. She picked the whole lot up and showed it to the girl. The trapped speck did not move.

'They're so thin,' said the daughter. 'One-dimensional.'

'Two-dimensional – that's so's they can move through the animal's fur.' Her mother squatted down beside the basin and held the glass over the water. 'I feel like a priestess or a magician or something. A new rite. Releasing the flea. Dah-dah.' She lowered the card partially into the water then withdrew it, leaving the flea floating. They both peered closely at it.

'Look at the legs – the length of them,' said the girl, leaning over the side of her bed. Her mother nodded.

'That's why they can jump over the Eiffel Tower.'

The flea was in a panic, cycling round the surface of the water, travelling backwards. The girl flopped back on her pillows, panting.

'Oh God,' she said.

'What?'

'That's really exhausted me.'

'Rest for a while.' The girl nodded. She was very white now.

'You've ruined my card,' she said. 'It looks all weepy.' The water had made the ink run. Her mother patted it dry against the carpet.

'It's an old one,' she said.

'I like to keep them all. Let me see it.' Her mother turned over the face of the card and handed it to her. It was a picture of a person in bed covered from head to foot in bandages. 'Oh, that's really ancient – two years ago, at least. From Johnny.' All the volume had drained out of her voice.

Her mother was bent over still staring at the flea.

'It's not floating,' she said. 'Surface tension. It's in a kind of dimple on the surface.' She looked up at her daughter but the girl didn't move. She just lay there with the card in her hand and her eyes closed. She could hear her breathing through her nose.

With her finger she sank the flea to the bottom of the basin and got up and tip-toed out.

About an hour later the buzzer rasped again and the mother went in.

'Could I have my tea now?'

'Anything to eat?'

'One bit of toast – no marmalade.'

When the supper was made she carried in the tray and set it on the chest of drawers. She pulled her daughter up into a sitting position, and propped her large sitting-up pillow behind her, then put the tray across her knees.

'Do you want me to stay?'

The girl shrugged. 'Whatever you like.' The wind rattled the windows and rain scudded against the panes. Her mother sat down on a bedside chair.

'It's a terrible night.'

The girl nodded and sipped her tea. The draught made her mobile rotate. A year ago, when she'd rallied slightly, she'd lain on her side in the darkened room and, with a little help from her father, had made a papier-mâché model of the sun. She was pleased with it. Then she made the earth and moon in the months that followed. When they were all finished she said, 'And on the seventh month she rested.' Now the heavenly bodies hung from the ceiling on threads above her bed. 'Give me something to stare at,' she'd said. 'Like a baby in her pram.' The earth was realistic, with blue oceans and brown-coloured land, but the sun and moon had faces. The yellow sun had spikes radiating from it and half the grey moon's face was covered in black shadow.

'How's our friend getting along?' said her mother. She looked towards the basin still on the floor.

'How does anything travel like that? It just hurls itself

anywhere. Doesn't know if it's going to land in the fire – or my tea or anywhere.'

'A leap in the dark,' said her mother and smiled.

'What a life.' She bit at the edge of her piece of toast. 'Well, it's over now.'

'So . . .' Her mother leaned back in the chair and joined her hands behind her head. From the quiet tone of voice the girl knew immediately what was going to be said.

'This has been a better . . . It's been a less bad month.'

'I don't want to talk about it.'

The girl chewed her toast – then leaned forward to take a sip of the tea. She always drank it hot with very little milk in it.

'Compared to this time last year,' said the mother.

The girl's voice was on the edge of tears so the mother stopped talking. Her daughter rubbed her eyes, then stared straight in front of her, still chewing.

'Where's Dad?'

'He took your wee sister to the pictures. Just to get out.'

'What's the film?'

'Something in the Odeon. With Matt Dillon in it.'

'He's amazing.'

The sun swung almost imperceptibly from side to side. The earth turned slowly to face the moon.

'Any time we got a flea at home,' said her mother, 'it was blamed on the picture house. I used to come up in lumps and Mum'd say, "When were you last at the pictures?" There was never any possibility that you could've picked it up in church.'

'Or school.' She lifted her tray off her knees and offered it to her mother. 'I'm too tired. I'll have to lie down.' She toppled her sitting-up cushion onto the floor and keeled over flat on the bed. Her mother set the tray on the dressing-table and sat down on the chair again. She said,

'Take it easy.'

After a moment the girl leaned over and looked at the basin on the floor.

'Where is it?'

'It's still there. Don't panic.'

'Give me the backscratcher.'

Her mother handed it to her. It was a stick with a small fake hand at the end of it, the fingers curled up. The girl dipped it into the water and tried to squash the flea between the plastic knuckles and the bottom of the basin.

'Love . . .' Again the quiet tone.

'Talking about it doesn't change anything.'

'It gives a purpose. Goals. Something to aim at.'

The girl had turned the plastic hand round and was now trying to cradle the flea in its palm. Every time she brought it to the surface the flea slipped sideways off into the water.

'What's the point?' she said.

'You're sick. You're twenty-one years of age. You've improved. Someday you'll be better. We have to prepare for that. Aim at it.'

'Huh.' She rolled her eyes away from her mother and looked up at the papier-mâché globes above her. 'Improved.' Her eyes filled with tears. Then she whipped the backscratcher down onto the surface of the water with a slap, splashing it over the carpet. She buried her face in her arm. She was half shouting words, half crying them – this is what talking about it does, she was trying to say. Her mother went to sit on the bed beside her and put an arm around her shoulder. The girl was shuddering and shouting into her hair and the crook of her arm and the tumbled sheets. Her words were wet and distorted.

'I'm not, I'm not,' said her mother. 'Not for one minute am I blaming you. All I'm saying is that this time last year –no, two years ago – you couldn't get to the bathroom on your own . . .' The mother held tightly onto her daughter's shoulder. It was sharp with thinness under the material of the football shirt. Eventually the girl stopped crying. Her mother went to the bathroom and damped a face-cloth with hot water and brought it to her.

'Crying doesn't help,' said the girl. 'Nothing helps.' The cloth steamed as it was opened. Her mother massaged her daughter's face. 'What time will Dad be back?'

'Ten? Half ten?'

The girl leaned out of bed, picked up the backscratcher again and began to stir the basin with it.

'Maybe don't tell him I was crying.'

'Okay.'

She withdrew the plastic hand and this time the flea was stuck to the back of it. She brought it up close to her face to inspect it, curling up her lip as she did so. Suddenly it jumped.

'It's alive,' she screamed.

'I don't believe it. It can't be.'

'It is.'

'God Almighty.'

Both women squealed and laughed with the shock it had given them.

'The flea jumped over the moon,' said the girl and continued to laugh. She lay back on her pillows, her shoulders shaking, her hand over her mouth. Her mother smiled and straightened out the coverlet. She bent over, her eyes only inches above it, staring.

'Right,' she said, ' – let's take it from the very beginning.' Her mother searched every visible inch of the coverlet but could see nothing. 'Don't worry – we'll find it before it finds you. It's only a matter of time.' She reached out and with a licked finger touched every speck.

'No.'

Every black particle.

'No.'

Any crumb.

'Definitely not.'

The girl listened to her mother's voice with closed eyes.

THIS FELLA I KNEW

This fella I knew – he spent his boyhood in a place between here and Sleivemish – out beyond the point there. On the outskirts of Lettermacaward.

And wait till I tell you this. He earned the best part of fifty pounds a day folding shirts.

And the best part of it was, he never folded a shirt in his life. His mother said he just threw them at his backside. But he was smart enough for being rared on a bit of a farm.

And he went to the University in Belfast. And did a degree in all kinds of things – engineering and physics and mathy-matics and God knows what.

And at the finish-up didn't he get a job across the water folding shirts. In a big concern. Marks and Spencer's, I think it was.

A new shirt, now, is an experience. And, before our friend with his University degrees got on the job, it was a dangerous one – for you could end up going out till a dance needing a blood transfusion, there was that many stabs in you from putting on the new shirt. That was until our friend came along – with the mathy-matics and the engineering. Folding, it seems, is a science. I'm told a bit of paper can't be folded more than eight times, no matter should it be a sheet the size of Ireland itself. Anyway, the aim of the thing was to get the shirt-folding down to the one pin. And this your man did – no bother.

And they paid him a powerful sum of money for the knack of doing this.

And, do you know, when he had earned his money nothing would do him but he'd come back home from England and buy himself a bit of land and put eleven cows on it.

But somebody had it in for him – for it didn't work out.

And didn't the cows get the grass-staggers and warble-fly and God knows what and he had to sell up the bit of land and go off again and concoct a scheme for bending cardboard boxes into hexagons for decorated chocolates.

But he was a smart boy, right enough, for he made money hand over fist at this and d'you know what I'm going to tell you – he was the boyo who came up with the idea of thin bits of square sweets, each one in its own brown envelope. Would you credit it?

And they became all the rage and the bosses at the factory went down on their knees when they heard he was leaving, but no – nothing would content him but to buy a farm of land he had seen advertised in the 'Dungannon Observer' just outside Gortin.

And all along, his mother had been mailing him the paper every week to England – in a brown wrapper. Wasn't that cute of her? To keep tabs on him, hoping to get him back one day.

Anyway, this time he stocked the farm with sheep and no sooner had he done it than they all got foot-rot and grooley stomach and that was him beat again – the lad had no luck whatsoever.

And it was back to the packaging. That's what they called what he did. Packaging, by God. The kind of thing you or I would do at Christmas – for nothing extra.

And they paid him a fortune for it. He became known in the trade as 'the man who could package anything' – and when your man packaged it – no matter if it was a bar of soft shite – it became a best-seller.

And money became a plentiful commodity. In the digs he was paying that much he could leave the light on all night without raising any hackles.

And every week he put some by and when he had enough ha'pence scraped together didn't he have a go at a bit of a farm for the third time. Serves him right, says you.

And this time it was the pigs. The fool gave up the job across the water.

And he comes back and buys a place beyond the bridge there. The Mammy'd be able to see him at half past ten Mass every Sunday from now on. He must have prayed the knees off himself or else the Mammy did. Because this time the boyo succeeds. And he starts making money hand over fist.

And buying that pink newspaper – and carrying a rolled umbrella from the house to the byre, if you don't mind, and wearing glasses even though he didn't need them – divil the bit – he could tell a full stop from a comma at the far end of the room. And having a mirror fitted to his bicycle instead of looking round like everybody else.

The difference between him and everybody else round here was packaging 'the product' – he wrapped it in cellophane and called it 'Bacon like it was before the war'.

And he sold everything but the grunt. The bacon itself, the pig's ears, the trotters, the curly tails – some said he sold the arseholes to school masters for elastic bands round the bundle of class pencils. Wasn't he the cute one too?

A FOREIGN DIGNITARY

The view from my window at the inn looked outward onto a small courtyard garden where everything seemed to be in bloom at once. The effect was quite, quite lovely. I watched a gardener stooping among the plants weeding, occasionally watering. Like everyone else here, he wore a buff-coloured smock. He had a bag of maroon powder which he was trowelling into the soil around the roots of the more colourful species. It looked like the dried blood fertiliser I use in my own garden at home.

The man raised his head and, when he saw me watching him, smiled in a gap-toothed manner. I nodded to him, not wanting to seem aloof, and staggered a little as I stepped back from the window. I had been warned about the period of adjustment one must go through at these high altitudes so I sat on a wicker chair until my dizziness passed.

Away from home like this I write a letter to my wife at least once a week, sometimes two if I find time heavy on my hands. The fact that they reach her months later, sometimes even after I have returned, is of little importance to me. After the day-long babble of strange tongues and dialects, in the quiet of my room I establish a communication of a sort with her. In some ways it is a similar activity to prayer, and even though there is no hope of a reply I inquire after our daughter, Elgiva. She is a young woman who is ill with a skin complaint which makes her avoid the company of all but her closest female friends. Her condition comes and goes for no apparent reason. The skin of her face and throat flare up into a dry angry redness in a patch whose edge is as irregular as a coastline. Her eyes become blood-shot and inflamed. Although she claims the condition is not painful it is pitiful for others to look upon. After her last attack my wife and I decided that it would be best to have all mirrors removed from Elgiva's rooms.

The Director of Prisons joined me for dinner at the inn. He was a small man with features typical of the region – a large hooked nose, olive skin, an unshaven look. His command of my language was almost perfect. Like everyone else he wore the buff-coloured robe. The only difference was that he had a medallion of some sort hanging on his chest.

He talked about each dish as it was presented, seeming particularly proud of one course containing sea fish. Coming from where I do this did not seem remarkable until I remembered that we were thousands of miles from any coast. And the transport, as I know to my cost, was lamentably slow. I cannot describe the discomfort I endured in getting to this place.

We were in an alcove slightly removed from the others who were eating and drinking. The Director pointed out various men of standing in the community but they all looked alike to me.

'It is a very popular place,' he said. 'All the more so when they know a foreign dignitary is here. They are curious to see you.'

'Dignitary indeed! I am a civil servant – doing my job.'

'A highly placed civil servant.'

'One who carries out other's orders, none the less.'

The Director of Prisons leaned towards me and whispered, 'It also means there will be entertainment.'

A small band of musicians began to play while we were having dessert. The sound was thin and, to my ear, quite quite raucous but I applauded loudly when they finished.

It was only when a young girl came out into the space between the tables that I realised she was the sole representative of her sex in that place. She began to dance to the music and again the Director leaned across to me.

'This is for you.'

She was very young, not long out of her childhood, and was dressed in a kind of long white folk costume. The dance consisted mostly of arm movements and gyrations of the hips – the feet moved but rarely. As she danced her eyes were downcast – which I found very alluring – fixed on the floor some inches in front of where I was sitting. Towards the end of the dance its character changed and the girl stood stock-still with her feet wide apart and began to ruck up her costume finger by finger. Past her shins, past her knees, above her thighs until she revealed her tiny dark pubes and buttocks. The men applauded and banged the tables. The girl dropped her costume and bowed to me, then turned and left. Everyone was now looking at me. The Director said,

'She is yours for the night, if you wish it.'

'No, really. It is kind of you to offer but I am a married man. And as you know, that is forbidden in our culture.'

The Director raised an eyebrow and shrugged as if he didn't believe me.

'If it is disease which worries you I can assure you she is a virgin.'

'No, really. Thank you.'

I offered to pay the girl some money lest she be disappointed at my refusal but the Director would not hear of it. He said that already she had been well rewarded.

I spent an uncomfortable night, sleeping only fitfully. I twisted and turned, thinking obsessively about the pleasures I could have had with the child dancer. I knew that as a representative of my Government I could not be seen to accept her and yet the child was so attractive. Visions of her little rounded buttocks, her scant hair below the paleness of her belly, kept me awake until dawn began to colour the room.

While at breakfast a note was delivered to me from the Director informing me that he would meet me before noon. I was amused at the mixture of formality and casualness of these people. When he arrived the Director bowed stiffly, yet apologised because we would have to walk to the prison. Someone had forgotten to arrange transport. I gathered my notebooks and papers and we set off together. As we walked the Director of Prisons insisted on carrying my briefcase.

'I hope you had a comfortable night,' he said.

'Thank you, I did.'

The pavements were in a state of poor repair and the roads rutted and broken. Many people sat at street corners begging, but on seeing the man with the medallion they did not put their hands out to us. They were emaciated, with the result that their eyes seemed to have grown larger. Our progress was watched by a slow turn of the head.

'Your Government have expressed great interest in our system,' said the Director.

'Indeed. Your crime figures are quite, quite remarkable.'

'The only real crimes are political. Everything else is . . .' He paused for a moment, searching for the right word. 'Venial? Misdemeanours which can be forgotten. The man who steals a cow is made to pay it, or its value, back; the murderer usually acts in the heat of the moment and we forgive him provided he makes a contribution to the family of the injured party. I will take you to the Courts tomorrow and you will see the process in action.'

'I very much look forward to that.'

We were moving into a better district. Laburnum trees with their delicate hanging blossoms lined the streets; we proceeded through a wide gateway into a garden of open aspect and thence towards a colonnaded walk.

'The philosophy of imprisonment is one that interests me,' said the Director. 'You can either punish, reform or protect. These are the options. There is no real need for the first one – punishment is very old-fashioned. The state should be above such a childish reaction. Although I agree with one of your famous writers – "The power of punishment is to silence, not confute".'

I could not quite place the quotation so allowed him to continue.

'And on the matter of reform, Councillors of the Courts can dissuade most people from committing another crime. Your prisons, I believe, are overflowing with petty criminals who will never change. All this is a great drain on the resources of a State.'

'But what if they offend repeatedly?'

'We have the ultimate threat of imprisonment. It is a great deterrent.'

I was becoming a little breathless and presumed it was the effects of altitude. I tried to hide my panting and asked,

'How far is it to the prison?'

'This is it,' he said. 'We are in it.'

I looked around. As I walked through the low colonnade, the place reminded me of a monastery more than anything else. There were two gardeners, one raking the grass he had just scythed, the other working with a hoe in the flower-beds.

'No walls? Not even a gate?'

The Director smiled.

'No.' He seemed to dismiss my incredulity because he went on, 'The one class of offender we have found who is NOT open to reform is the political animal – the revolutionary. He is a zealot who is . . .' again he seemed to be searching for a word, 'incorrigible, whose sole aim is the overthrow of the whole system and, quite logically, the system needs to protect itself against him more than any other.'

The scraping of our feet sounded in the arches of the cloistered walkway which met just above our heads. I was faintly aware of whispering or scuffling noises but did not want to be impolite and appear to be distracted from what my colleague was saying.

'If a tree is to be attacked by disease where would you afford the most protection? The branches, the bark or at its roots?'

'The roots, of course.'

'Exactly. Then we are of like mind.'

A perfume, as of night-scented stock which I have growing in my garden at home, wafted along between the pillars but there was another smell, not so pleasant, mixed with it like a base note, which I couldn't place. The scuffling or whispering became more audible and then I distinctly heard a voice speaking in a language I did not understand. I turned but could see no one. Behind me in a shallow drain I saw what I could only interpret as a piece of human excrement.

We turned at right-angles into another colonnade.

'The cost,' said the Director, 'is what interests your Government most.'

'Indeed.'

'There is a clemency caucus active in government who want the return of the death penalty for political crimes. But I do not agree. What we have here is maximum deterrent along with maximum protection for the minimum cost. Four men can run this whole prison by themselves,' he smiled, 'and still have some time for gardening.'

'Those two men are not prisoners?'

'No, the prisoners are here.' He indicated to my right. I looked and it was only then that I noticed the uprights which I had, up until that point, taken to be part of the structure of the cloister. They were shaped like tall broom cupboards.

'In here?' I asked. The director nodded. I stepped forward and, by rapping with my knuckle, discerned that they were made of metal.

'Iron,' said the Director. 'Treated in such a way that it does not rust.'

I looked at the blank face of the container, then examined the side nearest to me.

'Soldered shut', said the Director, 'and bolted to the stone. That is why we can afford to run the place with only four warders.'

'But how do you feed them.'

'The warders or the prisoners?' The Director smiled.

'The prisoners.'

'Each containment unit has a hole here for food.' The Director pointed to the side furthest from me. I looked at what he indicated and saw a small, square aperture about five feet above the ground. Something moved in the darkness inside. A face stared out at me. Whether it was the face of a horse or a human I could not tell. All I was conscious of was the whiteness of an eye. The Director pointed towards the ground and said,

'And a hole at the bottom for waste.'

'Remarkable. Quite, quite remarkable.'

We turned another corner into a similar colonnade where

the flat stones of the floor were shining wet. A man was operating a long jointed bamboo pole which gushed water from its open end. He was guiding the pipe into the upper hole of each containment unit and flushing it out. Soiled water rushed from the hole at floor level and ran down the channel into gratings. He was followed by another man with a wicker basket who was distributing food – what looked like hard balls of dark rice.

We did not like to interrupt this work, so turned yet another corner. Here I noticed that the containment units were much smaller and remarked on this to the Director.

'Political crimes run in families,' he said. 'In the more extreme cases we find it necessary to confine the whole family. The father may have planted the seed of revolt too deep to be rooted out.'

I asked if I might take some measurements and the Director agreed. I got out my tape and approached the nearest containment unit.

'This is a girl,' said the Director. He pointed to a mark on the metal. My curiosity about who was within was immediately aroused. As I measured I heard small scufflings inside. 'She has only been here since the beginning of the year.' When I came to measure the upper aperture I saw her face. Through the tangle of hair I could see she could have been a sister to the girl they had made dance for me the previous night.

'When women commit political crimes,' said the Director, 'they are a hundred times more virulent than the men.'

Then the prisoner turned to me and did a quite remarkable thing. She spat. I recoiled but the saliva caught on the material of my collar and I dropped my tape while searching for a handkerchief. The Director, apologising profusely, strode down to the corner and called one of his men. Knowing what was liable to be on the floor I picked the tape up with my handkerchief, rolled it all together and put it in my pocket.

The Director came back with the warder who had been scything the grass but who was now carrying a large sledge-hammer. He indicated the girl's containment unit.

'Excuse us,' said the Director. The man raised the hammer, swung it over his shoulder and, with all his strength, crashed it against the metal. There was a thunderous noise, as from the biggest untempered bell I have ever heard. It was deafening for those of us in the confines of the colonnade. What it was like for the creature inside I cannot imagine.

'Proceed,' said the Director and we turned and walked away, leaving the man swinging his hammer again and again. As we passed through the gardens back to the inn the sound echoed after us with monotonous regularity.

After lunch at the inn I excused myself to the Director, saying that I had to write up my observations and notes. I really wanted a nap because of my previous poor night's rest.

In the quiet of my bedroom I could still hear faintly the continual gong of the sledge-hammer. It occurred to me that the man swinging it must have reached the point of exhaustion and wondered if someone had relieved him.

Because of the noise, again I was unable to sleep. Instead I began a letter home.

O'DONNELL v. YOUR MAN

Mrs O'Donnell averred that a friend purchased a transistor radio for her and that she sat down to listen to it in Minchella's cafe in Paisley when the BBC was broadcasting a story written by your man; that her friend also purchased for her a bottle of ginger beer; that Minchella took the metal cap off a bottle of ginger beer, which was made of opaque glass, and poured some of the contents into a tumbler; that, having no reason to suspect that it was anything other than an everyday story she continued to listen; that she heard the word *fuck*; that when her friend refilled her glass from the bottle there floated out the decomposed remains of a snail; that she suffered from shock and severe gastro-enteritis as a result of the nauseating sight and of the fearful word she had just heard; that, having heard the word *fuck*, she could not unthink the word *fuck*; that, contrary to her normal vocabulary, it occasioned her to think of different parts of speech appertaining to the word: *fuckable, fuck-wit, fucker, fucking, fuck-bollock*; that in the same way she was unable to forget the impurities she had already consumed. She further averred that the short story was manufactured by the defender and broadcast by the BBC to be sold as entertainment to the public (including herself); that it *was written by your man and advertised in the* Radio Times *bearing your man's name. She also claimed that it was the duty of the writer and not the Broadcaster to provide a system in his compositions which would prevent fucks entering his stories – just as Minchella should have devised a system preventing snails from entering his bottles – and to provide an efficient system of inspection of stories prior to their being broadcast, and that his failure in both duties caused the aforementioned distress and sickness.*

What may listeners properly expect when they hear a story on the radio? The answer is surely not that it be free from such fucks as the author's care could keep out, but that, like dead snails in ginger beer bottles, it be free from fucks absolutely.

COMPENSATIONS

Ben, the younger boy, was copying down the football scores into the sports-page as a voice on the wireless called them out. His brother, Tony, sat with his ear almost against the loudspeaker. The boys' grandfather was reading the other pages of the paper. Ben felt he could guess the score from the high or low way the announcer said the team's name. When the results were finished the boys' grandmother spoke out from the kitchen.

'Well, Ben?'

'Where's the coupon?'

'It should be behind the clock.'

'It's not.'

'Wait now.' Grandma, drying her hands, came in and looked in the flap beneath the calendar. 'Do you think we've won?'

'No chance.'

'You never know. Somebody has to win them.'

'It'll never be us. We never have any luck,' said Tony and went upstairs.

She found the pools coupon beneath the bowl on the sideboard along with other bits of papers – printed prayers for a speedy recovery, novenas, the bread card – and handed it to Ben. The pools sheet was like the bread card – boxes of ruled blue lines.

She said,

'Wouldn't that be the quare surprise for them coming back?'

'No chance.'

'They could do with the money after paying for a jaunt like this.'

Ben looked at the grid of eight draws his grandfather had chosen and compared them to the actual results. The old man said it didn't matter about the teams – he just plumped for the same eight draws every week. Football know-alls never won.

'The first one's wrong.' He handed the results to Granda Coyle with a shrug and a shake of the head. The old man peered down at the sports-page through his glasses. He hadn't shaved well and had missed sandy white hairs at the corners of his mouth. Ben put the coupon behind the clock and asked,

'When's the tea?'

'Just as soon as I choose to make it.'

Grandma moved back out to the kitchen. She fried three eggs, scrambling them on the pan with a fork, and divided them into four. A slice of bacon each and soda bread which she'd baked earlier. The soda bread was always served dry side up hiding the bacon and egg. She set the four plates on the table.

'Sit over,' she said. 'And give your Granda a tap.'

Ben reached out and touched his grandfather's arm. The old

man looked out from behind the newspaper and saw the tea ready.

'Thanks,' he said. He unhooked the wire legs of his glasses from behind his ears and heaved himself to his feet.

Grandma opened the door and shouted up the stairs,

'Tony – Tony your tea's ready.'

Nobody spoke as they ate. Ben listened to the noises they all made. His grandfather's mouth was shut as he chewed but he breathed heavily down his nose. Grandma had a knob of gristle at the hinge of her jaw which sometimes clicked – like somebody pulling their knuckles. Tony deliberately opened his mouth to annoy Ben, letting him see the half-chewed contents.

'Stop that,' said Grandma.

'How long to go now?' asked Ben.

'Three days – it's past the halfway mark.'

'What day do they come back?' asked Tony.

'If I told you once, I've told you a thousand times. Wednesday.'

'What time?'

'How would I know. I'm not flying the plane.'

'What are they saying?' asked the old man, cupping his ear towards Grandma. She leaned forward and shouted,

'Just – when are they coming back.'

The old man nodded and stared at Ben.

'Wednesday,' he said. 'They'll be back on Wednesday.'

'Why don't you wear that hearing-aid of yours?'

'What?'

'Never mind. It's not important.' Grandma dismissed the whole thing with a wave of her hand.

The boys had been told that their mother and father had gone to France. They didn't know much about France – the only thing Ben knew was that French films were dirty so when his grandmother said they were on a pilgrimage he felt better. People went on pilgrimages to places in Ireland – to Knock and Lough Derg. One of the teachers in the primary school, Mister Egan, went to Lourdes every summer to help with the sick and the dying. Working in the baths, lifting the afflicted out of their wheelchairs, lowering them into the holy waters. Everybody said he was a saint – and they always remarked how he never got anything himself – no matter what diseases had washed off into the water.

The door bell rang and Grandma stopped chewing.

'In the name of God . . .' she said. She closed her eyes. 'Nurse Foley.'

'Well I'm off,' said Tony, wiping his mouth with his hand. 'I couldn't stand the excitement.'

Both brothers got up from the table. Ben went to open the vestibule door and Tony ran upstairs.

Nurse Foley smiled and walked down the hall past Ben.

'Hello Tony,' she called up the stairs at Tony's heels.

'Hi.'

When Nurse Foley came into the kitchen she said in a kind of aghast voice – 'You're not at your tea, are you?' Grandma smiled. Granda didn't even look up. Nurse Foley went and sat by the fireside facing towards the table. Before she sat down she smoothed both hands down her coat at the back of her knees to make sure she wasn't going to crease it.

'Take off your coat,' said Grandma.

'I'm not staying,' said Nurse Foley.

Granda made an excuse that he was going to get his hearing-aid and left the room. Nurse Foley was about the same age as Grandma and dressed in much the same way, except in black. Ben had heard that one of Nurse Foley's jobs was washing the dead. How could anybody do that? How could a woman do that – especially if it was a dead man. He looked at her knuckly hands unbuttoning her coat. There was a blue apron hidden underneath.

'Would you look at me. I took a last-minute notion to go to confession and I just dashed. Sure nobody'd mind the apron, especially Himself.' She rolled her eyes up to heaven.

'Would you take a cup of tea – there's plenty in the pot.'

'If it's going spare – I wouldn't mind.'

Grandma got a cup and saucer from the cupboard.

'A snig of sugar?' she asked, smiling.

'And just the one milk,' said Nurse Foley and gave a sort of laugh. Grandma passed the tea over to her.

Granda came back with his hearing-aid clipped to the front of his cardigan. Ben thought it looked like a small bakelite wireless. Sometimes when Granda tried to turn the volume up, it gave a shrill whistle and annoyed everybody, including him. He sat down in the corner and looked from one woman to the other so that the wire which led up to the flesh-coloured thing in his ear became more obvious.

'Was there many at confession?' asked Grandma.

'A good few,' said Nurse Foley, 'but there was three priests hearing. They were getting through them rightly.' The empty saucer remained on her lap as she sipped her tea. Grandma said,

'I meant to go myself. But it'll keep till next Saturday.'

'Och Mrs Coyle – sure don't I see you at the altar rail every morning in life.'

Grandma nodded, tight-lipped.

'There's some hard praying to be done.'

Nurse Foley shook her head in agreement and sighed.

'Any word from them?'

'Not a thing – sure a postcard takes ages. The best part of a fortnight. So I'm told.'

'I suppose so.'

Nurse Foley's face was solemn but when she turned to the boy she smiled.

'Well, Benedict – any luck with the pools this week?'

Ben shook his head. Grandma said,

'Divil the bit.'

'Wouldn't it have been great to be able to hand them the seventy-five thousand as they stepped off the plane,' said Nurse Foley. Grandma nodded her head and smiled a bit.

'It'd be a little compensation.'

'Och I know that – Mrs Coyle. No question.'

'But isn't it typical of you, Nurse Foley – wanting to win so's you could give it away to somebody else.'

'Acchh – sure what would I want with all that money.'

When Ben looked up at her she winked and laughed. Grandma said,

'It was good of you to lend them the suitcase.'

'I'm just glad to see it used. And where would I be going at my age?' Nurse Foley shook her head again. 'They've had no luck whatsoever. But maybe that'll change, please God. Only time will tell.'

'The Lord works in mysterious ways,' said Grandma.

'His wonders to perform,' said Nurse Foley. 'I just hope he can keep his strength up. Although how anybody eats the slime and muck the French eat I have no idea. Did you ever taste garlic? It would turn your stomach. And they put it in *everything*. Like the way we use salt here.'

'And snails, I believe.'

'What are you talking about – horses, Mrs Coyle. They ate horses.'

'Away – '

And then after a pause in which Grandma shook her head Nurse Foley repeated,

'Horse meat – how-are-you.'

'Och away . . .'

The fire crumbled and sparks flew up the chimney.

'Ben, get a shovel of coal.' Ben did as he was told and went to the coal-hole in the back yard. The new coals were damp and hissed when they went on the fire. Ben set the shovel outside the back door and came into the room again.

'And what about her?' said Nurse Foley. 'Do you think she'll cope?'

'I've never known her not to.'

'The flying – the strange food – organising and remembering everything – above all, the thing of knowing – it's a lot to ask of her.'

'Prayer'll see her through. Everybody is praying.'

'Only time'll tell.'

Ben looked at his Grandma and then at Nurse Foley as they talked. They seemed not to look at each other. Nurse Foley stared down sideways into the fire. Grandma stared up at the frosted top pane of the window.

'Have you your own prayers said yet?' asked Nurse Foley.

'No – always straight after the tea. As you know,' said Grandma.

'Sure I'll join you since I have the beads with me.' She took out her rosary from her apron pocket and eased herself off the chair to kneel down.

'Call Tony,' said Grandma to Ben and held up her beads and rattled them at Granda.

They all began saying the family rosary. When Granda knelt at the chair his hearing-aid was useless. He said his prayers into himself because he couldn't join in the responses at the right time.

Tony knelt by the door so's he could escape immediately it was over. Ben made sure he was at the chair with the paper on the seat. He read an advertisement for Burberry raincoats while they repeated the Hail Marys over and over again. There was a drawing of a woman wearing a raincoat and striding through rain which was just black strokes all going the same way. The woman's leg, with its seamed stocking, was reflected in a puddle. Ben thought about washing a dead girl. The thought leapt into his mind and he couldn't get rid of it. A soapy flannel able to move anywhere. He tried to be good and put the thoughts out of his mind. He was getting a hard-on and if he allowed the thoughts to stay it would be a sin. In the middle of the rosary – it would be double the sin. He tried to concentrate on the prayer.

'Holy Mary Mother of God prayfrus sinners now and at the arovar death Amen.'

Beneath her armpits. Around her belly button. The wet face cloth moving down between her legs.

'Ben, can you not kneel up straight?' said Grandma. 'You're bent over there like a pig at a trough. The Second Joyful Mystery – The Visitation. Our Father who art in heaven . . .'

He turned his body away from her in case she would see what was happening to him and knelt up straight with his hands joined. He looked at the ceiling. He tried not to think of washing the body of a girl. Then he would definitely know whether they had hair hidden down there or not – or whether his brother was trying to make a fool out of him. Tony was smart. Tony knew everything. But Ben had seen marble statues in books with nothing obvious down there. What he did know was that they had hair under their arms. Last summer a French girl student had come into their class to teach for a while. On hot days she wore a summer frock and when she pointed out things on the blackboard they all saw the hair in her armpits.

He had to think of something different.

The worst thing he had ever seen in a paper was the air crash of the Busby Babes. The snow on the wreckage of the plane carrying Manchester United back from Munich. The thought of Duncan Edwards, his favourite player, lying dead. And all the others. It was beyond crying.

What if the plane bringing his Mum and Dad back from France crashed? That would make him an orphan. It was the first time they had ever flown and they'd seemed very nervous leaving.

'The Fifth Joyful Mystery – Jesus is Found in the Temple. Nurse Foley?'

Nurse Foley began giving out the prayer.

'Our Father who art in heaven . . .'

He thought for a while of being an orphan. Maybe it would be good. Everybody would make a fuss of him. Giving him extra things. But the thought of both his parents being dead was unendurable. Either one of them, maybe. Sometimes he made himself choose. Mum or Dad? Which was worse? Who would he miss the most?

After the rosary proper they said all the trimmings – right down to a prayer for a special intention. His Grandmother would never tell Ben what it was – it would ruin any chance of success if she said it out loud. And he noticed that when she said this prayer she clenched her eyes tight shut and moved her lips more than she usually did. When everything was finished Grandma blessed herself and kissed the cross of her beads and hung them on the handle of the cupboard. Tony left the room immediately and they heard him pounding up the stairs.

'I suppose Lord Duke McKittiax has better things to do than listen to us gabbing away,' said Nurse Foley, sitting back up in her chair and putting her beads in her pocket. Granda continued kneeling at his chair, not realising that the prayers had finished. Ben tapped the old man's shoulder and he looked up a bit startled. He smiled at Ben and said he was doing some extra praying – a wee prayer of thanksgiving for Celtic winning.

'That Charlie Tully's something else.'

Grandma had begun to clear the table, stacking the dishes up on the draining-board of the sink. The two women talked as Grandma went to and from the table. Granda fell asleep with his head lolled to one side and his mouth open. When Grandma had finished clearing the table she covered him with an overcoat to keep him warm. Nurse Foley asked,

'How's he keeping this weather?'

'He's rightly. The pains bother him a bit – but touch wood he's been fine today.'

'Surely they'll bring back some Lourdes water. You can put a drop of that on his joints.'

Grandma turned to Ben who was sitting pretending to read the paper.

'Ben, why don't you go into the other room and amuse yourself.'

'There's nothing to do.'

'There's those dishes to be done.'

'I'd better be on my way,' said Nurse Foley.

'Stay where you are. The dishes can wait.'

Ben lowered his head closer to the paper.

'I know there's nobody better than Our Lady when it comes to that kinda thing', said Nurse Foley, ' – but did they ever think of McHarg?'

'McHarg?'

'Seventh son of a seventh son.'

'Where's he?'

'Beyond Randalstown somewhere. It's nearer than France and it could do no harm.'

'I haven't heard of him.'

'It might be worth a try.'

Granda stirred in his sleep and made chewing noises. The coat began to slip off him and Grandma leaned over and adjusted it.

'His ears is beginning to flap,' said Grandma, nodding at Ben. 'Why don't you go and play some records, son?' Ben made a face and moved out of the room. As he closed the door he heard them lower their voices but did not listen to what was being said. He never listened at a door in case he heard something bad about himself.

He considered going up to talk to Tony but he would be reading or pretending to read. Going to Grammar school had changed him a lot – it had given him a big head about himself. He liked showing off – trying to scare everybody, quoting stuff like *Beware, beware the Ides of March* in a hoarse voice. Ben hoped to get his Eleven plus and be able to join him after the summer. It would be good if they had to walk to the College together.

In the sitting-room it was a grey summer's evening and the window panes were covered with rain. Away from the fire it was cold. There was a damp patch of wallpaper on the chimney-breast caused, so his mother said, by some cheap-skate builder patching a hole with 'weeping sand' and it became more obvious on wet days. The noise of traffic passing was in that room all the time and somewhere a blackbird was singing. When a certain type of double-decker bus went past, the window pane vibrated, shaking the droplets of rain. There was a fly somewhere but he couldn't see it.

The chiming clock on the mantelpiece had stopped long ago because the key to wind it up had been lost. Ben stood staring at it. It had Roman numerals which turned more and more upside down the nearer they got to half-past.

He lifted the clock down and set it on the rug. There was a long hat-pin with a black pearl handle beneath where the clock had been and he took this and lay down. He opened the door at the back of the clock. Inside, a row of tiny brass hammers. The chimes were made of brass rods of different lengths. With the hat-pin he lifted and dropped each hammer onto its chime. The echoes went on and on and on – the different notes interfering with each other until the noise of traffic came back. It was the saddest sound he had ever heard. If he lifted all the hammers and released them slowly by withdrawing the hat-pin then it sounded like a harp – unearthly. Like heaven. Deliver us from evil. He played the clock because there was nothing else to do. Once, when he was much smaller, a visitor had asked him if he played anything and when he said – the clock – they all threw back their heads and laughed. He smiled but he wasn't sure what was funny.

When he tired of the clock he went over and looked out at the street. The bluebottle flew into the window bizzing against the glass. The sound stopped and it climbed slowly. Ben folded a paper record sleeve so that the central hole became a bite out of one side. He folded it again so that the bite disappeared and it became a strap of paper.

After a while the fly zig-zagged back into the centre of the room and flew in squares around the light bowl. You could see a freckle of dead flies and moths in the bowl when the light was turned on. Eventually the bluebottle buzzed to the window again and Ben whacked it to the floor where he stamped on it. When he took his foot away the fly bounced against the pile of the fawn rug.

In the street a woman walked beneath her umbrella so that he couldn't see her face – just a coat and legs. He put his hands in his pockets. The face of a dead girl might be covered with a sheet – pulled up from her grey feet until only her face was hidden. Everything else he could see. He felt the beginnings of a hard coming and took his hands out of his pockets again. His eye kept being drawn to the dead fly on the carpet. He scooped it onto the record paper and threw it in the fireplace. Against the black of the grate he couldn't see it.

He went out into the hall and heard the voices still going on and on. His father had modernised the doors – hiding the panelling beneath hardboard – so that it made a double thickness. The voices were murmuring – indistinct. They were up to something. If he opened the door they would stop talking. They would look up at him waiting for him to give a reason for his being there. He hated that.

He went back to the front room and plugged in the radiogram. It was a huge unfinished affair being built by his father – 'a genuine piece of furniture'. The wood inside had not been varnished yet and smelt like freshly sharpened pencils. To the right of the turntable was a pile of records without their paper covers. They made zipping noises as he sorted through them. He played *Whispering Hope* very low – it wasn't the kind of thing he should be playing. Far too sloppy. If his brother caught him he would laugh at him and taunt him. Why do you play that when Johnny Ray's there? So he lay down with his ear very close to the black cone of the loudspeaker. His father had not got round to covering the speaker with material. *Whispering Hope* made him want to cry, it gave him a strange feeling in his stomach. Two voices, a man and a woman's, threading in and out of one another. Harmonising. Later he played Johnny Ray singing *Just-a-walking in the Rain* and turned the volume up loud.

Grandma banged the sitting-room door with her fist and shouted,

'Turn that thing down a bit.'

Nurse Foley opened the door and said at the top of her voice,

'That's me away.'

Ben turned the volume down. Nurse Foley stepped into the sitting room. Grandma stood behind her. Ben could see that they had both been crying.

'The spit of him,' said Nurse Foley. She reached into her pocket and produced a half crown and gave it to Ben.

'It's not seventy-five thousand but it'll get you some sweets.'

'What do you say?' said Grandma.

'Oh thanks – ' said Ben.

'Don't look so surprised,' said Grandma.

'But what's it for? It's not my birthday or anything . . .'

'It's for being good,' said Nurse Foley.

ST MUNGO'S MANSION

Your man opens this letter and reads about the plight of St Mungo's Mansion and how it's going to be bulldozed if nothing is done about it. Well, the people who have written your man the letter are going to do something about it. No messing about for them. They plan to publish a recipe-book.

The implication is that your man is a celebrity or, if not that, then at least someone prominent in public life and they not only want a favourite recipe but an anecdote as well. For reasons of copyright the recipe should not be identical to any in an existing publication. So your man rolls up the sleeves.

Dear Sir, says he, my favourite is a boiled egg in a cup. Wrong. Better again is two boiled eggs in a cup.

METHOD

1. *Insert two raw eggs into tap-water contained in a saucepan and heat to boiling point. Maintain this temperature for four minutes.*

2. *Separate the shell from the edible part. Protection for the hands may be necessary here – heat-proof gloves of some sort. Put the edible part into a cup – add butter, salt, paprika and*

pepper to taste and smash it about with a fork or something. Eat with the best of soda bread.

My favourite anecdote about myself is not really an anecdote. It is the title of a story. There is no story, only a title. It is: A THREE-LEGGED HORSE CALLED CLIPPITY.

Hope the above is helpful to saving Saint Mungo's Mansion. Yours sincerely, Samuel Beckett.

Your man is not really Samuel Beckett but it amuses him to think he is.

JUST VISITING

The pub, almost opposite the hospital gate, had an off-licence attached. He waited a long time for the green man before crossing. The rain was falling constantly and the wind darkened the pavements as it gusted. He ran with his coat collar up. A bell chinked when he opened the door and a girl came out from the back to serve him. There was not a great range of Scotch in half bottles so he bought, not the cheapest – because that would look bad – but a middle-priced one. The girl began to wrap it in brown paper.

'Don't bother,' he said. 'It'll do like that.' He slipped the half bottle into his jacket, making sure the pocket flap concealed it.

In the lift to the wards a Sister with winged spectacles stood opposite him. He thought he heard the liquid clink in the bottle when they stopped at any floor but she didn't seem to notice. When the lift doors opened on the fourteenth floor he smelled the antiseptic – but there was another smell – a perfume he couldn't quite place. A sweet, intense – uneasiness. He walked along the corridor.

He hadn't seen Paddy for three years – not since he himself had moved to the city. Through the ward windows he could see men in various propped positions, in beds, on beds. A sign above one – NIL BY MOUTH. Was that him? How much had the illness changed him? Would he recognise him easily? A nurse in her forties sat at a desk mid-way along the corridor. She continued writing her report, then looked up.

'Just visiting,' he said. 'I'm here for a Mister Quinn. Mister Paddy Quinn.' She stood up and escorted him. The name tag on her lapel said *Mrs MacDonald*. Again he was aware of the liquid clinking in the bottle in his pocket.

'He's in a room by himself – he's still very weak after his operation. So please – if you don't mind – don't be too long.' She opened the door and called out, 'Visitor for you, Paddy.'

A figure lay flat in the bed with his back to the door facing the window. The visitor moved round the bed to face him.

'Paddy – how are you?'

The nurse closed the door. Paddy gave a groan and heaved himself onto his elbow.

'I hate that bitch, MacDonald. She is so fucking patronising,' he said. 'Good to see you, Ben.' Ben reached out and touched the older man on the shoulder. 'Watch me – or I'll fall apart.' Ben plumped up the pillows and wedged them behind Paddy's back.

'So – how are you?'

'Some fucker unseamed me from the nave to the chaps.' Paddy lay back on the pillows and blew out his breath. His beard and hair were now completely white. When he opened his pyjama jacket to display his wounds Ben tried not to let anything show on his face. There was an incision beginning at Paddy's neck which zig-zagged down his side to the bottom of his ribs.

'Jesus, it's like the map of a railway track.' There were junctions and off-shoots and either there was extensive bruising or else the whole wound had been painted with iodine.

'It's hand-stitched,' he said. 'Nothing but the best.'

'Is it sore?'

'Naw . . .' Paddy looked at him. 'What the fuck d'you think?'

Ben nodded, not knowing whether to smile or not.

'Did you manage to run the cutter?'

Ben glanced over at the small window in the centre of the door. There was no one looking.

'In my wash-bag,' said Paddy. Ben slipped the bottle from his pocket into the wash-bag, covered it with a damp face-cloth and zipped it up.

'Crinkle-free,' he said. 'The girl was going to wrap it but I said no. I didn't know the lie of the land up here.' The wash-bag was now stowed at the bottom of the bedside cabinet. Ben sat down on a chair. Paddy leaned back on his pillows.

'It's good to know that's there.'

'Are you not allowed *anything*?'

'Two cans of Guinness a day. Three if someone's brave enough to buck the system.'

'Slim rations,' said Ben.

'I'm on that many bloody drugs . . .'

'When did you arrive?'

'The night I phoned. They operated the next day.'

'I'm sorry I couldn't get up sooner but you know how it is.'

Ben shrugged, making out he had no control over anything. 'So – how have you been since I last saw you?'

'Apart from cancer – okay.'

'Sorry – but you know what I mean. How's the town I love so well?'

'The terrible town of Tynagh. It's not been the same since you left. Morale has taken a nose dive.' There was a long silence. 'Where green peppers wrinkle on the Co-op shelf.' Ben rested his elbows on his knees and stared down at the terrazzo floor. Paddy stared at the white coverlet. 'What's the teaching like here?'

'For fuck's sake, Paddy . . .' Ben leaned back in his chair and appeared to concentrate on the ceiling. There was another pause – the wind buffeted the window and the rain sounded like hailstones against the glass. 'I mean – they wouldn't operate . . . to that extent if they didn't think they could . . . I mean the signs are *good*. My own father – they just took one look and closed him up again. Told my mother the only thing left was to take him to Lourdes. Are you getting radio-therapy?'

'Chemotherapy. They say it's worse.'

'But they wouldn't put you through all that if they thought . . . if they didn't think you had an . . . excellent chance.'

'Did she take him? To Lourdes?'

'Yeah.'

'And?'

'He died the week he came back. We were just kids – didn't even know he was ill.'

'Fuck it – pour me some orange juice. In that glass.' There was a carton on the grey metal locker and Ben stood and began to pour out of the torn spout of the cardboard. 'Stop – go easy. Just enough to colour it.'

'What?'

'The whiskey.'

'Are you sure? Paddy, I'd hate to be the one . . .'

'I'll do it myself then.'

'Stay where you are.' Ben crouched and took the half bottle out of the wash-bag. There was a series of small metallic snaps as he broke the screw-top, then the hollow rhythmic clunking as he poured whiskey into the tumbler of orange juice.

'Say when.' Ben kept his body between the tumbler and the door. He stopped pouring. Paddy said,

'When.'

He put the bottle back in the wash-bag and handed the glass to Paddy. Paddy sniffed at it.

'Terrible fucking smell – orange juice.' He raised the glass to his mouth, quickly tipped it back and swallowed half its contents. Then the remainder. He lay for a moment with his eyes closed. 'Oh that's good. What about yourself?'

'No, it's too early for me. Thanks all the same.'

'That's how it all started. Difficulty swallowing. It went on for a couple of months – and then it got so bad I went to Doctor Fuckin Jimmy. And now I'm here.'

'Doctor Fuckin Jimmy.' Ben shook his head, stood up and sniffed at the air. 'Maybe I'd better open that window for a bit.'

'Jesus, you'll have it as cold as the caravan in here.'

'It's the smell – if the nurse comes in.' The lower section of the window hinged in at the bottom. The wind gusted up into his face when he opened it. 'It didn't stop us having some good nights.'

'Plenty of internal central heating. Days in the *Seaview*, nights in the caravan.'

'Good times, Paddy.'

'Laughing to piss point.'

'*Mine's a whiskey*,' said Ben, imitating Paddy's voice, '*and I'll leave the measure up to yourself.* And when it came to your round, you oul bastard – *What kind of beer can I buy you a half pint of?*'

'That's a lie.' They laughed and nodded.

'Do you still live in it?'

'The caravan? Yeah. If it hasn't blown away. It should be tied down a day like that. But I can't be bothered any more.'

'Come on Paddy . . .'

'The doctors were saying – when I get out the District will *have* to house me. They say they'll not release me *until* I get a place to recover in.'

'You see – they expect you to get better.' Paddy nodded but he didn't seem sure. He said,

'How's the wife and weans?'

'Fine – everybody's fine.' Ben looked at the racing grey sky and then down at the leafless trees in the grounds.

'I liked the kid who thought wind was made by the trees waving.' Ben looked round and Paddy was lying back on his pillows with his eyes clenched shut. 'Maybe I'd better go,' he said. 'Is there anything you want?'

'Yeah – you could run the cutter for me again. In fact, if you don't I'll break your legs for you.'

'Okay – okay. But it'll be Friday before I can come.'

'And close that fucking window.'

Ben snapped the wood frame back and snibbed it.

'The windows must be like that to stop you jumping out. When it all gets too much.' Just then Mrs MacDonald tapped the glass of the door with a fingernail. 'I'm overstaying my welcome here.'

'Fuck her. I remember seeing it written up in big six-foot letters once – on a wall. *Do what you're told – REBEL.*'

'So you keep telling me.'

'She's nothing but a saved oul bitch,' said Paddy. 'Before you go I want you to do something for me.'

'Yeah sure.'

It seemed important and he leaned forward to listen attentively. He thought of wills, of funeral arrangements, of last wishes.

'See the wardrobe – there's a dead man in my dressing-gown pocket. Dispose of it.'

On the way out in the main corridor he smelled the sweet intense perfume again. It was so strong it almost caught the back of his throat like cigarette smoke. Mrs MacDonald was now sitting at her desk in the light of an anglepoise. He stopped and waited for her to pause in her writing.

'Yes?' Mrs MacDonald looked up from her work and Ben felt he had to point vaguely in the direction he'd come from.

'I've just been visiting Paddy Quinn.'

'Of course.'

'And I wanted to give you my number – just in case. He hasn't anybody. Here, that is.' She wrote down Ben's particulars.

'You're a friend of his?'

'Yes – we've known each other for about ten years now. We were neighbours – sort of.'

'In Tynagh?'

'Yes – when I was teaching at the High School there.'

'Lucky you. What a beautiful place. It's my favourite seaside town.'

'How do you know it?'

'Mr MacDonald and I drive through it most years. On our way somewhere.' Ben nodded but decided to say nothing. He cleared his throat.

'How is he? I mean I know he's weak but . . . how is he?'

'Mr Milne – sorry, the surgeon – is convinced that he caught it in time. They are all quite hopeful.'

'That *is* good news.'

'But he's almost sixty – and hasn't treated himself as well as some.'

'Thank you – thank you anyway for all you are doing.'

Then he saw the source of the perfume – behind Mrs MacDonald's desk – two bowls of hyacinths. Big bulbs sitting proud of the compost, flowering pink and blue and pervading the wards and corridor with their scent. It was a smell he hated because he associated it with childhood, with the death of his own father. A hospital in winter brightening itself with bowls of blue and pink hyacinths – a kind of hypocrisy, the stink of them everywhere. His mother crying, telling them all to be brave.

*   *   *

It felt like the first day of summer – warm with the sun shining out of a cloudless sky and the trees in the hospital grounds in full leaf.

When Ben went into the ward it was empty. Mrs MacDonald said with a repressed sigh that Paddy was probably in the smoking-room. Ben walked to the far end of the corridor and looked through the small window of the door. There were four or five men inside. He went in.

'How're ya,' he said. Paddy was in his wheelchair sucking his pipe.

'On fortune's cap I am not the very button.' They laughed. After the treatment the hair on the right-hand side of his face had fallen out and gave his beard a lop-sided look. He was fully dressed in trousers and jacket and sat apart, looking out the window. The others were in a group, smoking cigarettes. 'Have you put on some weight?'

'According to the scales,' said Paddy. The room was bluish with smoke and smelled stale. There was a green metal waste bin quarter filled with cigarette butts. 'And how are you?'

'Great – the first week of the holidays. Like the first couple of hours on a Friday night.'

'You can hardly see out this fucking window for nicotine. Look at it.' The glass was yellowish, opaque. 'It hasn't been cleaned for months. Nobody *ever* sweeps the floor in here. The message is, if you smoke in this hospital we're gonna make you feel like shit because we're going to treat you like shit.' He knocked his pipe out into the bucket and began to roll some tobacco between his hands. Ben sat down. The white-painted window sill had tan scorch lines where cigarettes had been left to burn.

'Take it easy – maybe in a . . . a ward of this nature they have a point.'

'Fuck off, Ben. People get hooked on things.' He tamped the tobacco into the bowl of his pipe and began lighting it with a gas lighter. 'Addiction is a strange bastard. It creates a need where no need existed. And satisfying it creates a pleasure where no pleasure existed.'

Ben looked at the cigarette smokers. At least two of them looked like winos, with dark-red abused faces. They wore hospital dressing-gowns over pyjamas and had open hospital sandals. Ben stared down at their feet. They were black like hide with pieces of cotton wool separating the toes. Their toes looked dried, encrusted and brittle. His eyes flinched away.

'Let's go outside. I'll take you for a spin in the wheelchair.'

'Did you run the cutter?' Ben nodded and indicated his pocket. 'Let's stash it in my room first. And I'll get you the money.'

'Don't worry about it. It's a gift – this time.' Ben wheeled him along the corridor. Mrs MacDonald was on the desk and she spoke to Ben as they passed.

'He's fair putting on the pounds,' she said. Ben felt obliged to stop the wheelchair. He nodded.

'It'll be food – you must be giving him food.'

Paddy sat staring ahead.

'Why don't you go out – that lovely day. Get a breath of fresh air.'

'It's not fresh air I want,' said Paddy, 'but the good fug of a pub somewhere.'

'Don't you dare,' said Mrs MacDonald and Ben and she laughed. Paddy's knuckles were white on the armrests of his chair.

Ben slipped him the half bottle and Paddy stood up and went into the toilet with it. He tried to vary the places he stored it. Ben stood waiting, staring out the ward window. Mrs MacDonald passed the door with a slip of paper in her hand. She smiled and stopped. She put on a whispering voice.

'I'm serious about that.'

'What?'

'The pub business. It would be terrible to undo all the good work. I'm holding *you* responible.' She grinned and walked away in her flat shoes, flicking at her piece of paper with her finger.

When Paddy came out of the toilet Ben smelled the whiskey off his breath as he got back into wheelchair.

'How much weight have you put on?'

'A couple of pounds but I'm still lighter than when I came in. It's that fucking chemotherapy-therapy that goes for you. And the no drink laws. They stop you drinking and then ask you to put on weight – for fucksake. Drink's full of calories.'

'I've been thinking about half bottles – the shape of them. There's something Calvinist about them. They're made flat like that *for* the pocket. No bulge, no evidence. A design to fit the Scots and the Irish psyche.'

'Shut up and drive.'

There were many patients outside in the hospital grounds, sitting on benches in pyjamas and dressing-gowns tilting their faces up to the sun, or being wheeled about. A couple of female nurses in white uniforms lay on the grass. There was a blackbird over by the railway cutting singing constantly.

'It even feels like summer,' said Ben. They stopped at an empty bench beside a laburnum tree and Paddy got out of the chair onto the bench. He sat filling his pipe, staring at the cascades of yellow blossom.

'This bastard's poisonous. You've no regard for my health at all.'

'What was wrong with those guys' feet – in the smoking room?'

'Gangrene – smoking makes your legs drop off.'

'What?' They both laughed. 'That's crap. Why doesn't it happen to you?'

'I guess I'm just lucky. Naw – it happens mostly to cigarette smokers. It's called . . . some big fuckin name. It stops the circulation to your feet. They go black and drop off.'

'And those guys are still up there smoking?'

'You've never smoked Ben, so shut your mouth.' He lit his pipe with the gas lighter and exaggerated every gesture and sigh of satisfaction. 'It gives a selected few of us a little pleasure as we funnel our way down the black hole to oblivion. Speaking of which . . .'

'What?'

'Why don't we go for a drink?'

'Naw – '

'At the clinic where they used to dry me out they *taught* me to drink. They said . . .'

'Never drink on your own.'

'And now *you* are here. It can't be too far to the nearest pub, for fucksake. Isn't there one just at the gate?'

'Naw – '

'What the fuck's wrong. Are you on the wagon or something?'

'No – it's inadvisable. It's very pleasant here.' A train rattled through the cutting but they could not see it. The blackbird changed trees and began singing from the opposite side of the tracks. 'So – any word of a house yet?'

'No.'

'Or any word of them letting you home?'

'No.' His pipe wasn't going well and he knocked it against the spokes of the wheelchair. 'Fuck it.' He sucked and blew but couldn't free the blockage.

'There's no need to go into a huff, Quinn.'

'The first time in twelve fuckin weeks that I get a chance to have a drink without those nurses breathing down my neck – and you won't take me.'

'That's right.' There was an ornamental flower-bed with bushes and grasses screening them from the front of the hospital.

'Pull me a bit of that stuff,' said Paddy pointing to stalks of wheat-like grass. Ben glanced in the direction of the hospital then did what he'd been asked. Paddy pulled his pipe apart and pushed the stalk through the plastic mouthpiece. When it was cleared he blew through it and reassembled the pipe. He threw the grass stalk on the ground at his feet. It was black with tar.

'*WHY* will you not take me?'

'Because you're not allowed. The doctors do not allow you.'

'What doctors have you been talking to, for fucksake?' He turned away from Ben in irritation and looked towards the hospital gate. For a moment Ben thought the old man might attempt to make it on his own.

'They serve coffee on the ground floor. We could go over there.'

'What doctor said I wasn't allowed to go to the pub?'

'Look, Paddy – do you want to get better or not?'

'That is not what we are talking about – we are talking about going for a fucking pint and maybe a chaser in a nice atmosphere with maybe a barmaid.'

'Paddy – catch yourself on. Do you not think I know you of old? Nights spent in the terrible town of Tynagh. Once you get into a pub there's no way of getting you out.'

'You're chicken. A coward. A man who can't break the rules no matter *who* lays them down.'

Ben stood up and ushered Paddy back into the wheelchair.

'Come on. I'll buy you a coffee.

Paddy got unsteadily to his feet and almost fell into the chair. He was shaking his head in disbelief.

Ben got the coffees in wobbly plastic containers and brought them down to Paddy by the window. Outside was a small lawn with more off-duty nurses, both male and female, sprawled on it.

'Aw fuck,' said Paddy, staring out. 'Lift your knees a bit more, darling.'

'Stop it. Would you like a biscuit or anything?'

'No.'

The formica table-top was covered in brown sugar spilled from a half-used paper sachet. The plastic container was too hot for Ben's fingers and he left it to cool. A baby was crying somewhere and two children were running up and down between the tables chasing each other. A mother stood and called them to order. Paddy stared out the window, his hands joined across his midriff. Ben began wiping the spilled sugar into a neat pile with a paper napkin.

'I sometimes do what they told you not to,' he said.

'What? Who?'

'The drying-out clinic. I drink on my own. At night.'

'Thank God you fucking drink sometimes.'

'When everybody's gone to bed.'

'You mean your wife.'

'I *like* to relax with a dram.'

'It'll not do you a button of harm. There are worse things,' said Paddy. The nurses on the lawn got up simultaneously and moved back into the hospital. Paddy looked up at Ben. 'I believe you're the undercow of that wife of yours.'

'Nonsense, Paddy.'

'Do you drink more or less when she's there?'

'Probably less. But I only have one or two.'

'Or three? Or more? When you're drinking you can only count to three.'

Ben smiled.

'Sometimes it's frightening to see the level on the bottle the next day.'

'You're not too bad then – if there's any left in the bottle. But it'll get worse – you know that. You're no fool, Ben.'

'Thanks for the advice, Holy Father.'

'I want you to remember this – you can only give advice to fools.'

'I don't understand.'

'If you feel the need to give someone advice you're *assuming* that they are a fool.'

'That is advice.'

'What?'

'What you're giving now – to me.'

'It's not advice. We're having a fucking conversation.'

Paddy pulled out his pipe and lighter. He pressed the plug of tobacco deeper into the bowl and aimed the flame at it.

Ben fanned his hand in front of his face to keep the smoke at bay.

'Problem drinking,' he said, 'is a thing that builds up gradually.'

'Problem drinking? What are you talking about *problem* drinking for?' Paddy laughed out loud. 'Drinking's the solution, for fucksake.'

'Paddy, you're right beneath a *No Smoking* sign.'

'Fuck it. People like the smell of a pipe.'

'In a hospital?'

'*Especially* in a hospital.'

Ben finished his coffee and made movements to stand up. 'Look I'll not be able to make it three times a week from now on. I have stuff for summer school. I'll come Tuesdays and Saturdays, if that's okay with you.'

'Yeah, sure. It's good of you to come at all.'

'Naw – . It's good to hear your crack again.'

'It's not the way it used to be. More's the fuckin pity. Ben, you're the best friend I ever had.'

'Easy on, Paddy. Statements are in danger of being made here.'

'No – it's true.'

'Okay – okay. But I've gotta go.' Ben stood up and spun Paddy round in the wheelchair and headed for the lift. There was no one else going up. When the doors closed Ben asked,

'Any dead men you want me to get rid of?'

'Naw – there was a fella got out yesterday. He took them away in his suitcase. They sent him home to die. But he took the empties all the same.'

* * *

There was snow on the hills which turned to sleet as Ben drove down into Tynagh. It was more a village than a town – a collection of shops, five pubs and as many churches all gathered around a harbour which had silted up over the past two decades. The school where he'd taught looked even more dilapidated and cement grey than he remembered. Because of the holiday the car-park and playground were deserted. On the football field in the drifting rain a flock of seagulls stood just inside the penalty area.

The hospital was on the far side of the town – on the outskirts. It shared a building with an Old People's Home. He recognised the nurse on the front desk; she had been a pupil of his. He remembered her as a bright girl – she had written a good argumentative essay on *The Nature of Tourism*. When she recognised Ben she blushed.

'Hello, sir. I presume you're here to see Paddy. He talks a lot about you.'

She led him down the corridor, speaking over her shoulder to him. He felt she was embarrassed at having made the slip and called him *sir*.

'So how are you liking the big smoke, then?'

'Oh fine – it suits me fine.'

She stopped outside a room and dropped her voice. 'They sent Paddy back here to . . . recuperate . . .'

'And how's he doing?'

'Not as well as we would like.' She gestured to the room and

186

continued walking along the corridor. She had an Elastoplast between her Achilles tendon and her shoe.

Paddy was lying on his bed against a pile of pillows with his eyes closed. There was a drip above his bed and a tube taped to his arm. His cheek bones stood out and he was a very bad colour.

Hearing someone in the room he opened his eyes.

'For fucksake Ben, what are you doing here?' His voice was hoarse and he seemed to have difficulty swallowing.

'Visiting you.' Ben reached out and shook hands. He was aware of the sinews in the older man's handshake. The arm with the drip attached lay flat, wrist upwards on the covers. 'You're looking okay – for a man that's been through the mill.'

'Do you think so?'

'I *know* so.'

'Jesus, I don't feel it.'

'What's it like here?'

'Fuckin terrible.'

'But you're surrounded by people you know . . .'

'That's what I mean. Nosey cunts on zimmers.'

The room was on the seaward side of the hospital and the windows had been dulled by the salt blowing off the Atlantic so that the grey-green of the hills looked even greyer.

'Is your wife with you?'

'No – it's just a quick visit. I didn't know whether you wanted me to . . . y'know, run the cutter.' Ben tapped his jacket pocket and pulled the neck of a half bottle into view.

'All very acceptable,' said Paddy. 'The more the merrier. Put it there.' He indicated the open shelf on the bedside cabinet. Someone had brought him a basket of fruit which was still covered in cellophane. The white grapes were beginning to go brown. Ben reached over.

'Where?'

'Anywhere.'

It was only then that Ben noticed the full tumbler standing on the bedside cabinet. He bent over and sniffed it. It was whiskey.

'They allow you it in here?'

'A little,' said Paddy. Then he smiled. 'As much as I can drink.'

'Is that a . . . That must be a good sign.'

'They say if it helps put on some weight it'll do no harm. Would you like a snifter?'

'Nah – Paddy. Never during the day. Anyway, I'm driving the car.'

'How long are you staying?'

'I'll go back tomorrow. All things being equal.'

'What the fuck kind of an expression is that? From an English teacher? *All things being equal.* When was any fucking thing ever equal?'

'Sorry. Sloppy speech.' Ben smiled. 'Any word of a house?'

Paddy shook his head. 'They say I've got to put the weight back on before I go anywhere.'

'Are you eating much?'

Paddy looked up at the drip and licked his lips. 'Lancashire Hotpot.'

Ben didn't know what to say. 'Sorry?'

'You remember we once talked about problem drinking? Well I've got it now.'

'What?'

'A problem drinking. My fucking throat's given up. I can't swallow anything any more. This is high protein, high fibre, high fucking God knows what – but it might as well be Molly Magill's pish as far as my weight's concerned.'

'Paddy – don't be so impatient. You're looking . . . okay.'

'Okay?'

'Okay is good enough – at this stage.'

'Angela says they put the apple tart and custard through at the same time as the hotpot. And a cup of tea.'

'Angela. That's it. I'd forgotten her name. Angela Stewart. She was a pupil of mine.'

'So she tells me.'

'Is there anything you want? Anything I could get you from the town?'

'Naw, thanks. When I was in the best of health there was nothing you could get me from this town.' He picked up the glass and took a tiny sip then lay back on his pillow. He held the whiskey in his mouth but some of it leaked out at the corner of his lips.

'What brought you to this godforsaken dump in the first place?'

'It's where I ended up. After the war. As good a place as any. As bad a place as any.'

'Oh aye – the Morse Code business.'

'For the North Atlantic. The trouble with drinking cronies is – remembering what you're told them. *Drink is a great provoker of four things* – the one Shakespeare left out was amnesia.'

Ben had to lean forward a little to hear what Paddy was saying. He took the glass from Paddy's hand before it spilled and replaced it on the bedside cabinet.

'I still like the taste of it,' Paddy said. 'So you've met Angela?'

'Yeah.'

'She's a great kid. She does things for me. I suppose it's her way of telling the matron to get stuffed. The rules do not apply to a man in my position.' His breathing was becoming difficult. He reached out for his pipe which lay in a tin-foil ash-tray. He sucked the mouth-piece but did not light it. 'Could you maybe call her for me?' Ben rose quickly to his feet.

'Are you okay? Is anything wrong?'

'Don't fuss, Ben.'

He found Angela at the front desk and told her that Paddy wanted her. This time he made sure to use her name.

'I'm very busy,' she said. 'Tell him I'll be along as soon as I can.'

'Thanks, Angela.' Ben sat with Paddy for another fifteen minutes. The older man was tired or drugged and kept dozing off. Ben didn't like to disturb him and sat saying nothing. The hospital was full of noises – there was a distant rattling of dishes, someone whistling, a plastic door flapped shut, in the next room someone dropped a pair of scissors in a stainless steel sink. When Angela arrived breathless, Paddy said,

'Here comes the upwardly nubile.'

'Paddy – what do you want this time?' She turned to Ben. 'He's a terrible bloody man. You see what I've to put up with?' Ben nodded and smiled.

'I want to have a drink with my friend here,' said Paddy. He indicated the bedside cabinet.

'What do you take me for? A bloody waitress?'

'You know what I'm talking about, sweetheart. And I want you to pour one for that teacher of yours. A large one.'

'Honestly, Paddy, I've got the car.'

He sat bolt upright in the bed and his eyes bulged. His voice was as loud as he could make it.

'Fuck you and your fucking car.'

Angela winked at Ben and poured him a glass of whiskey.

'Do you take water in it?'

'Indeed I do. The same again.'

The nurse handed him the glass and said to him, 'The toilet is on the left at the bottom of the corridor.'

'Sorry?'

'Just a little walk – for a few moments.' She raised her eyebrows and smiled.

'Oh yes – ?' He walked down the corridor and went to the toilet even though he didn't really need to go. When he came out Angela passed him, hurrying back to her post.

'He'll be in better form now,' she said.

Ben went back into the room. With one hand Paddy was combing back his white hair.

'There's your drink,' he said. Ben took it and toasted him.

'Cheers,' he said. He was looking for Paddy's glass to chink. The tumbler stood empty on the bedside cabinet. Paddy saw him looking and said,

'It's in the Lancashire Hotpot.'

Ben looked up at the drip. 'You old fuckin bastard.'

Paddy laughed. His eyes seemed brighter. 'All my life I've been looking for bad company to fall into and it's only recently I've realised I'm it.' They laughed a bit. 'I should've got Angela to fix one of these up in the caravan years ago. With a catheter out the window. You wouldn't have to budge for weeks.'

They talked about the good times – remembered the after-hours drinking, the windowsilling their way home, the parties with no food and 'the night of the starving fisherman' when they found bite marks in a bar of Echo margarine. When Paddy laughed it turned into a phlegmy cough which was difficult to stop so Ben tried to change the conversation and keep it as low-key as possible. After a while Paddy said,

'When you see people like her – Angela – it makes everything worth it. She doesn't give a fuck what anybody says.' He seemed to doze a bit, then jerk awake. He was beginning to slur. 'There was a thing about Wittgenstein on last night – on the radio – his last words were – *Tell them it was wonderful*. I think he was probably talking about the rice pudding.'

After about a half an hour Paddy felt into a deep sleep. Ben put his almost full whiskey where Paddy's tumbler had been. Then he left on tip toe.

* * *

Ben walked along the school corridor into the carpeted office section. The red light was on outside the Principal's office so he went into the Secretary's room.

'Hi Ben.'

'Who's in with him?'

'A parent – I think.' She checked a notebook. 'Yes, Lorimer of 3D – his father.'

'Can I see him next?'

'Doubt it, love. There's a Revised Arrangements in Geography Higher Grade meeting at eleven.'

'Lunch time?'

'Come down again at one – I hope you had a good night somewhere, Ben?'

'Why?'

'You look like you're a bit hung over.'

'I was at home. I'll explain sometime.'

'Cheers.'

Ben wasted most of his lunch hour waiting for the red light to be switched off. He went again to the Secretary.

'Who's in?'

'Nobody, love – just knock. He's probably at his lunch.'

Ben knocked.

'Come in.'

The room was filled with the scent of a single hyacinth in a pot by the window. It was that time of year again. The Principal was sitting behind his desk which faced the door. He was eating a sandwich and a cup of tea steamed on the polished surface of the desk. Beneath the cup was a wooden coaster, so crude it was obviously made by a pupil. The slats of the venetian blinds were half closed. Outside the harsh sunlight created a glare.

'Ben – what can I do for you?' The Principal was a dark silhouette. There was a distant yelling from the play-ground.

'Em – I got the news last night that a friend – a very close friend of mine . . . Well, that he died.'

'Oh, I'm sorry to hear that.'

'Yes, we got to know each other in the terrible town of Tynagh.'

'Oh yes – when you were teaching up there.'

'He was a great man.'

The Principal set his half bitten sandwich on a serviette on the desk. 'And . . . ?'

'I just wanted permission to go to the funeral.'

'When is it?'

'Tomorrow.'

'In Tynagh?' The Principal considered this for a moment. 'What you're really looking for is leave of absence.'

'Yes.'

The Principal sighed, 'It's sad but you know the rules as well as I do. The Region will only allow it for *close* relatives.'

'This man was a close friend. Maybe he's the father I'd like to have had.'

The Principal folded the paper napkin over the sandwich. He put it in the desk drawer and closed it. He cleared his mouth of food.

'I'm very sorry, Ben. It's not up to me. I can only make recommendations to the Region. The decision is not mine. And I can only make recommendations with regard to *close* relatives. If you like you can submit a request to the Regional Director.'

'And if he refuses?'

The Principal lifted his shoulders in a long shrug. 'Then you can't go.'

'He was important to me. More than a relative.'

'I'm afraid it can't be helped.'

'What would happen if I went anyway?'

'If you went awol?'

Ben nodded. He was still standing in the middle of the floor. The faint yelling from the playground seemed to grow in volume.

'That would not be a good thing – at all. Because we are very short-staffed at the minute.' He looked up at Ben, then swivelled a bit in his chair. 'With this flu that is going about.'

'He was called Paddy Quinn. And he was one of the best read people I ever met. He was sharp and he had very little luck.'

The Principal stood up. 'They say it's not a particularly bad flu.' He went to the window and changed the tilt of the venetian blinds so the room was flooded with light. 'Ben, if you'll excuse me, I have a lunch to finish.'

The funeral service was at ten o'clock and there was to be a gathering in the public bar of the Seaview Hotel afterwards. A piper had been engaged and paid for by the owner of the hotel as a mark of respect for a valued customer and friend. There was no point in Ben sending condolences – who would he send them to? Paddy would understand – he never did have any regard for ritual or the niceties of any situation. He would have said, 'Fuck it – do what you want to do.' At 9.45 Ben set his third-year class a comprehension exercise to keep them quiet.

'Sir, why do we have to do this crap?'

'Lorimer – you are supposed to be on your best behaviour. You do it because I say you do it.'

Ben sat, glad of the silence he could impose. When it came to ten by the clock and the class were working quietly he got up and went into the book cupboard. Although he preferred whiskey he had filled his hip flask with vodka – he knew it couldn't be detected on the breath – and he drank a toast to Paddy. Then another one. It was the first drink he had ever had during working hours and it made him feel good that he was, in some small way, giving them the fingers. He closed his eyes and leaned his head against a stack of *Art of English IV* and tried to visualise what was happening two hundred miles away in the town of Tynagh.

LOOKING OUT THE WINDOW – II

Lately your man has been doing a lot of staring out the window trying to catch who's dumping the rubbish. After the bin men there is nothing. Then, the next time he looks there is a poly-bag beside the lamp-post. He knows the pile will increase day by day. Bags marked Safeways, Boots, Top Shop. Then dogs will come and, intrigued by the contents, take them out and inspect them. Then piss on them.

Enough is enough. Your man creates a poster on white waterproof card with Indian ink which says

THIS IS NOT A DUMP;

RUBBISH WILL BRING

ABOUT VERMIN

He waits until nightfall and sets his poster beside the lamppost and the mountain of poly-bags.

The next day he is interested to see the reactions of passers-by. A young girl strides past and doesn't even notice it. He feels spurned. Maybe it is not in a prominent enough position. Perhaps red ink would have been better.

Suddenly your man realises 'To bring about' is a very

specific verb. To cause to happen. Rubbish would not cause rats to happen. What he meant was that rats would be lured to this area. Covered in shame he dashes out and looks this way and that. Seeing no-one he takes his poster back into the house. He selects another blank card and writes

THIS IS NOT A DUMP;
RUBBISH WILL BRING
VERMIN ABOUT!

He is unsure about the exclamation mark. To be on the safe side he removes it with white correcting fluid. It is better, less cluttered.

He waits for the dark before reinstating the poster. This time instead of setting it on the ground he tapes it to the lamppost at eye level. That night he has difficulty sleeping – so anxious is he to see the reaction of tomorrow's passers-by.